To: REGAN & PAULI...

BEST OF LUCK

A Corporate Move

(Power Never Naps)

A Corporate Move

(Power Never Naps)

Charlie Kitchin

ISBN 978-0-557-40220-5

Dedications

First and foremost to my parents that set the stage for me to move through most of my life so far with relatively mild setbacks and enormous successes. To my wife Lori for over 30 years of marriage and my two sons Josh and Charlie who have brought the reason for life into perspective over the years and certainly brought me the happiest times in my life. It always seems to amaze me when I look back over my life now in my mid fifties how fortunate I truly am. When I read history or read the current news it bewilders me how some people are so fortunate and some people are so unfortunate. The ups and downs at "The Corporate Move" reflect the operations at any small or mid-sized company in America and Canada in the last half of the 20th century and the first part of the 21st century.

I would also like to thank many people I have had the pleasure to work with and learn from over the majority of four decades. It is difficult to pick out just a few people, but I feel the need to at least mention a few. The most influential being John Dodd's who is one of my former bosses and certainly a mentor that influenced thousands of people in a positive way and allowed many people to become successful through their own hard work. I would also like to mention two more individuals that brought enlightenment for me over several decades. Doug Wynne and Doug McIntyre were both subordinates and colleagues with me in some very intense situations and many rewarding outcomes. These three people are the only ones I still communicate after twenty five years with thousands of people in the same company. In the end we all have very few people that are true friends.

In the corporate world many people pretend to be your friend for many different reasons. Many other people have influenced this book, and may understand how they did it, when they read this book. This is a fiction novel based on many dreams, perceptions and many real life experiences.

Introduction

The book covers activities and perspectives that may or may not have happened in the 60's, 70's, 80's, 90'and the 2000's. Some characters are based on personalities that I came in contact with over the years. Other characters are based on a combination of personalities I have at least met and more likely I knew at least some of them well. In retrospect, I did not really know the majority of them at all.

The story picks up the lives of characters after they have been on the planet for some time. Every character brings different strengths to the new venture and unfortunately many weaknesses as well. These individuals are attempting together to form a company that has great product potential and a noble cause that will be a positive influence for society in general. Hopefully readers will identify with many of the individuals and can relate some of them to personalities in their own world.

Nobody wants to walk alone through life. Yet, in many respects we all walk alone through this life. Many of us get caught up with our own agendas and literally won't allow other personalities to get a place inside our own personal bubble. Friend's and relationships in the corporate world are two different animals. We as humans tend to mask them because of agendas and somehow get our brain to merge the two. Thinking they are the same thing is a huge mistake. They are not the same thing and shouldn't be. If you are the boss most everybody will want to be your friend. Even if you are not the boss most associates will want to try to be your friend. All those relationships are just that relationships. If you believe these business relationships would continue if you were no longer employed at the same company you are sadly mistaken. As I said in the dedication of this book after almost 25 years at the same company I now communicate with three of the associates I worked with all those years. It gives you an empty feeling that you spent so much time and so much energy on attempting to be-friend people at work. Business is business and attempting to make it be a friendship environment blur's the experience and usually diminishes productivity. Understanding this does not mean you have to be guarded with associates rather just be aware that they rarely if ever will put your best interest above or even equal to theirs. Understanding this will improve your productivity and allow you to manage better if you are a manager. If you are not the boss, understanding these concepts will help you manage the personalities around you in the work environment. Even quality managers run amuck because they are competent to manage others, but forget (or don't know) you have to manage up, down and sideways. Managing your boss and even their boss as well as your colleagues in the business is as important as and possibly more important than managing subordinates.

It's normally always a wild ride in any corporate environment but some are more exciting than others. At the new company (The Final Result) the ride can be downright thrilling. Throughout the story readers will hear from Norman the dog. Norman's perspective points out the truth in many cases and often cuts through the human personalities that are attempting to stay in their own personal bubble. Some people put agenda's over anything else and are truly going through life alone although not many of them would understand or admit to it. These people in Norman's mind are part of the dark side of reality.

Table of Contents

Chapter 1

Setting the Stage

Ryan Oxbow was a fairly normal kid from a fairly normal family living in America in the second half of the 20th century. Going through twelve years of parochial school tainted his rebel soul and set the stage for the rest of his life. Following high school Ryan went on to community college and was as bored with college as he was in high school. After 15 plus years in middle management for a large American corporation Ryan was yearning for a new adventure and to get out of the job that had become mundane.

With his rebel soul in full march Ryan decided to go off and try to make his mark on society and improve his own economic future. Ryan was a six foot, 170 pound guy and had a little more than grey hair around his temples. Ryan teamed up with Denny Connor an old high school buddy that had gone off to The University of East Carolina and had come back to the Northwest and bounced around for some 15 years working for both small and large companies using his machinist talents. Ryan spent the same 15 years and had risen in the ranks to Vice President which was considered upper management in the largest rental company in North America. Ryan and Denny had spent high school basically joined at the hip. Even though they had spent 5 years apart while Denny was away at college, when he returned to the Northwest they picked up where they had left off and had many social activities in common.

The quality time Ryan and Denny spent together wind surfing and now kite boarding in the Columbia River Gorge had made the bond between the two very strong again over many years. The other quality time Denny and Ryan spent together happened at Ryan's folk's house. Ryan's parent's house was a custom built home in a fairly ritzy neighborhood in South West Portland. Ryan's dad designed and had built the homestead some 30 years ago, but it still was very comfortable and stylish. Ryan's mom had basically redone the place about every 10 years. Mr. and Mrs. Oxbow (which was the way even Ryan and Denny still addressed Ryan's parents) were known for the festive parties they threw several times a year. This was the only house Ryan could remember as he was 8 years old when the family finally moved in. The house was over 4,000 square feet with 5 bedrooms and three bathrooms and took over two years to complete. The grounds where amazing with many different species of plants and trees that Ryan's mom had planted over the years. The property was just over 2 acres with a big stand of fir trees at the North end. Having over two acres inside the city limits even 30 plus years ago was a coup for any family. Ryan's earliest memories were playing with toy cars in the dirt around the foundation of the new house. Every time Ryan came or went from the house he would always pause for a minute and recall the great times he had making dirt roads for all his toy trucks and cars. Ryan's mom still had them in his old room as she kept all the kids rooms about the same as they where went they flew the coup.

Denny never had much of a family and spent many nights at Ryan's parent's house over the past 15 years enjoying Ryan's mom's home cooking and the atmosphere of family. During grade school and high school Denny pretty much lived at Ryan's house every weekend. Denny lived with his mom during grade school and high school in an apartment above the pharmacy down on the main drag almost two miles away from Ryan's folk's house. Denny and Ryan both had gone to the same Catholic grade school and high school, but that was the only thing that the two families had in common. Denny's mom passed away the first year Ryan was at East Carolina University from a chronic disease she had battled for years. Denny never knew his dad or any grandparents and his mom never married. She worked as a clerk at the pharmacy off and on when she was able in exchange for apartment rent. The guy that owned the building was a softy and was happy to give Denny and his mom a place to live.

Many times over the years Ryan and Denny had discussions over many beers about starting their own company. Ma and Pa Oxbow where very old school and had grown up in Milwaukie Wisconsin and had come out west to Portland after World War 11. Much of the ethics both Ryan and Denny had where rooted from Ryan's parents. Ryan's dad's name was Charles and his mother's name was Navona. Charles was a structural engineer and had worked for an engineering firm in Portland for 30 years. Ryan's mom was a high school teacher that taught English. Nona as she was called was a deeply religious Catholic and getting every one of her kids successfully through the Catholic high school she worked for had been a main goal of hers over many years. Ryan was the last of her 4 kids and as it turns out the hardest one for her to reach her goal but she got it done. Charles was a staunch republican with a very fiscal conservative attitude. Ryan's dad never was religious but liked the discipline that the Catholic education system seemed to have. Denny was almost like another kid for the Oxbows threw out the boys high school career. Fast forward 15 years and you get the following scene.

Charles having to put down the family dog (an 8 year old husky/Sheppard mix) because he had bad hips. The dog named Zip could not get up from a sitting position without help. The picture of Ryan's dad carrying the family dog to the car for his final trip to the vet had burned itself into the brains of both Denny and Ryan.

Ryan and Denny were together that day at Ryan's parent's house in South West Portland, Oregon. As Ryan and Denny watched they promised each other right then to start a company that would create not only income for them but also allow them to parlay there income into something really significant for society. It was paramount in both of their minds to help these aging dogs have longer fulfilling lives and give owners many more years with their beloved partners. Through many twists and turns, as there is no direct path to wisdom, Ryan and Denny fought through back doors, side doors, and an amazing amount of arrogant individuals. That is where the story of "A Corporate Move" begins.

Ryan and Denny had always loved animals in general, and dogs specifically. They shared many memories of taking dogs to the beaches and woods as they were growing up. Denny had a solid education in animal anatomy through his major in biology. Ryan had a natural ability to put things in place to make things happen. Over the many years of management Ryan had refined his skills in handling people and the goofy personalities.

Denny and Ryan formed a small LLC company named "The Final Result" doing business as "Uplifting Puppies". Their business plan was to create a helping hand machine that would help older dogs stay more mobile. Denny had been working for years theoretically on a prototype of a harness system that could electrically generate lift on demand. The next step would be financing the start up. Denny was very mechanically inclined and with his knowledge of anatomy was able to piece together a concept of a harness that could allow lift on demand. Denny had played around with this concept all the way back in his college days. Over the past 15 years he continued to work in his garage on a prototype. It was not until Denny showed Ryan the rudimentary prototype that the concept of helping older dogs was the application that the prototype needed. Up till then Denny was trying to find an application for the lift but nothing had clicked that was marketable.

In order to raise capital Ryan and Denny each chose someone to target on the project that would bring both capital and contacts to the table. Enter Eileen House and J.D. McGraw. JD was big man and at the age of 56 he still had the stature of a much younger man. He was an old boss and mentor of Ryan's and not only brought capital but also contacts in the financial arena. Eileen was an old college buddy of Denny's (yes they had a fling) she had gone onto post graduate studies at Stanford after her undergraduate studies at East Carolina. Eileen trusted Denny as did JD with Ryan and both of them thought the project had great potential. JD stood on many other boards at other companies and had numerous governmental contacts that could be looked to for additional capital in the future. Eileen was currently a vice president of a highly successful software firm but also had family money that she was interested in investing. Eileen had long wanted to do something on her own after so many years of making products and money for someone else. JD always liked Ryan because he was one of the few people he could depend on doing exactly what he was instructed to do. JD was impressed with the presentation of the concept. Eileen always trusted Denny but was not totally convinced until Ryan gave the presentation to her.

Both JD and Eileen infused the little LLC with 250,000 each. No one knew Ryan had the backing of his dad except JD. JD and Ryan's dad had known each other for many years. Charles made a deal with JD to back his money if everything went to hell. Ryan did not even know about the side deal. No legal paperwork was developed but JD and Charles both knew there handshake was better than any document. Ryan's dad thought it better to have Ryan answerable to JD instead of answering to him. The stocks for the initial LLC where issued and the beginning rolls showed;

> Ryan Oxbow-126 shares
> Denny Connor-126 shares
> JD McGraw-124 shares
> Eileen House-124 shares

All four principles where elected as the first board of directors. Ryan took the President's position and headed up the marketing division while Denny took the Chief Financial Officer position and headed up the research and development division. The original corporate office started at 530 Ash Street and amounted to a rundown leased building with just over 10,000 sq feet of warehouse space in a very seedy part of the city. There was a 7-11 down on the corner with Stark Avenue. Stark was a main arterial on the east side of the city. Ash Street ended just two blocks from Stark and had two old two story buildings that were formerly used as shipping and distribution centers for toys from China on either side of Ash. Filling in the other parcels on the two block street where overgrown bare lots and two towing companies with storage yards on either side of the street. All in all, it looked like a pretty grim landscape but Denny and Ryan figured it was cheap and they did not currently envision a retail division for the company. They scavenged enough office furniture to get started and spent heavily for machine equipment and IT infrastructure. The first hire that Ryan made was to get an accountant on the team to do some forecasting and help create some presentations that would make sense to any bean counters.

Enter Terry Gwen. Terry was a tall thin gal with a real shapely figure even after having four kids. Terry had done her undergraduate work at the University of Michigan and Masters work at Princeton. Ryan had met Terry in New York socially when Ryan was working in the city for nearly five years before he went back out west. They had kind of stayed in touch over most of the last decade trading Christmas cards and e-mails. Terry had moved out west after a ten year stint with a formidable accounting firm in New York. She did not want to go back to work in a high intensive environment so she and Ryan worked out a deal to work for them about half time. Terry had a really good separation agreement with her past employer and was more interested in her recreation activities and her kids than money. That worked great for the company currently and would give Terry and Ryan justification to cut out early every once in a while and get in some kite boarding. Terry was forty and had four kids and a husband that worked from home and loved being a house husband. She did not need to work but wanted to at least keep her feet wet in the business world. She longed for more passionate work but hated the "pressure to produce" corporate environment. She hoped that this current opportunity would be a good match. She really wanted to get involved with an entity and have involvement, but with less pressure. Ryan set out with Terry and Eileen to get some initial presentations down on power point to present to market. Denny with Eileen's help had already bought (mostly on credit) some machines and the fledgling start up had the software and hardware to start working on a prototype.

Denny and Eileen where both great with software and computer hardware but they needed some expertise in the actual machining tools end of producing a prototype. They put an employment ad out on a local Craig's list and received only one applicant for the machinist position. Doug Batter had held several machinist positions milling metal parts but had no experience with robotic parts. Doug seemed like a likable guy that had held down jobs for years at a time and his resume did not have any unexplainable gaps. Doug was a tall drink of water with a slender almost gawky looking body. After checking Doug's references Denny decided to give him a chance. This one decision may have been the best decision made early in the company's start up stage. Doug dove in full speed and in very short order had set up the first production line for the company. As time went on they nick named Doug "the hardware store". In an almost uncanny way he would come up with whatever was needed – 90% of the time without leaving the production floor. Often times he made the tool or part because there were no suppliers of the part or tool needed. Even though Doug had no college education he was so smart and inventive that he was contributing just as much or more than anybody on board. For example, getting the small gear mechanism to mesh properly with other gears he handmade a prototype gear (forged it in his own garage) that the suppliers could identify and replicate on a mass basis.

During the same time Denny, Eileen and Doug where building and developing the prototype harness Ryan and JD where setting up contact lists of potential buyers as well as mining for some other individuals for future funding. JD had the ear of a Wall Street executive Chance Law that was outwardly interested in the project and was talking huge amounts of money. JD was not a fan of Chance Law but nor was he able to ignore the funding he was talking about. JD took Ryan to lunch with Chance early on and they seemed to hit it off. During subsequent meetings JD continued to slow peddle Chance's proposals stating that the reputation Chance had was one of a takeover specialist that left companies and bodies in the wake of his takeovers. During one meeting with Ryan, JD and Terry presented a proposal for Chance to indeed invest in the company but issue no shares to him. Instead it was a straight forward loan that would pay Chance 8% on his money over a ten year period. During a meeting with Chance later in the week JD, Ryan and Terry presented the proposal. Chance, having graduated from Florida State and gone on to law school at Harvard, was no dummy. Chance was a short stout man with a bushel of gray hair. He looked and dressed kind of like a miniature Colonel Sanders. As time went on Chance would often show his little Hitler small man syndrome. Chance was incensed that he would have no real stake in the business. The meeting ended up civil but at this point the deal with Chance was shaky at best at least on the loan front.

Other options were starting to show some signs of hope including some very low rate loans from the small business association. In order to pursue these Ryan brought on Becky Germane who had been a great grant writer for many years and operated her consulting business on the side even after accepting her position at the company. Becky met Ryan at a trade show some 10 years ago and they had developed a strong relationship over the past decade. Becky would call Ryan from time to time to get his feedback on one thing or the other. Ryan and Becky thought along the same lines as far as business goes and they never thought of themselves as anything but business associates. Becky turned out to be a smooth operator and quickly brought in capital of nearly a half million on short term low rate loans through past contacts. They always say there is a ton of governmental money available but she was one of the few that could actually find it. Still no investors were on board with the weight of what Chance's proposals talked about.

Ryan and JD had begun discussions with several potential end user's including a large pet store chain, and a supplier of equipment for a large network of veterinarians. Ryan began to push Denny to produce a prototype that he could use as a demonstration model. Denny did have a rudimentary harness that he and Doug where trying to get working. The pressure of start up costs was beginning to worry Terry and JD and the company needed to start producing a revenue line projection that had meat on it. Most of the lenders to this point were held at bay by contracts that had no cash payments for the first year. The company had invested more than half of their capitalization funds to date on machine tools and parts and computer hardware and software. The balance sheet for the company was beginning to look grim and Terry began to set off alarm bells to all the principals.

Ryan had several potential customers that had been presented the product electronically but now they were demanding demonstrations. The graphic electronic presentation was impressive and very easy to distribute via e-mail. Eileen was able to produce an animation program that described and displayed a conceptual harness on a virtual dog. This presentation had been sent to 29 different companies and produced responses from 5. It was time to put up or shut up. Denny and Doug had the prototype working but insisted on at least six more weeks of testing. The harness was working as designed, but the control system that manages the harness was hard to operate. The actual harness uses electrical input to assist in lift for back legs. The harness only weighed 10 ounces using primarily light composite parts. The hand held controller was the size of a normal remote control unit. Now the company needed a dog to do testing on the harness.

Eileen had an older boxer that had hip problems. His name was Norman and he was just a pleasure to have on the team. Norman had been by Eileen's side since he was 6 weeks old. She had always wanted a dog and during the time she was volunteering for the local humane society eight years ago Eileen and Norman met and developed a precious bond. As time went on at the shelter she finally decided one day that Norman would not spend another night at the shelter. Norman had been in the shelter for three weeks and the next day he was going to be on the euthanized list.

Through all the testing, Norman took everything in stride. The harness could adjust easily to dogs 25 to 100 pounds. It did take sometime for the dog to adapt to accepting help from something he does not understand. After several weeks Norman felt comfortable with the harness and was accepting it as normal-Doug nick named Norman "Normal Norman". Norman was now ready to be the show dog for the demonstration team. The problem controller was now holding up everything and the pressure on Denny and Doug to get it right was now reaching disturbing proportions.

Denny and Doug where so frustrated with the control issues that they on their own gave up on the controller and turned their attention to having the harness be self activating. This of course was a completely different business model from what Ryan and JD had been marketing. On top of that it was going to be another long road down the research and development road including an additional testing period. Doug and Denny both new that it was going to be a rocky road, but they had just hit a wall with the old controller. Doug and Denny thought a harness that was activated by animal input would be more marketable because of the ease of use. They went on outwardly telling everybody that they were still trying to work out bugs in the remote. Finally, Ryan confronted Denny by himself to ask him what exactly where the bugs left to solve. Denny finally broke down and told Ryan what was really going on. Well the shit hit the fan front and center and everyone in the organization got sprayed with their fair share.

Ryan was livid, and as soon as the information got distributed throughout the company the moral of the team would become nonexistent and the future of the company could be in jeopardy. JD may have been the only one that mentally was able to move forward. JD had seen this movie many times before and intuitively knew it had only two outcomes, death or more capital. JD briefly met with Ryan in the hallway to try to calm him down. Given the choices, JD said "we need to focus on the Chance deal again". And so it was, Chance Law returns to the picture. Terry was considering resigning as she could see the bleak balance sheet ahead for the organization with no product to sell. Ryan was dismayed and the friendship with Denny had been stretched past the breaking point.

Eileen stayed out of the shouting matches but was equally dismayed at the current situation. Eileen was worried not so much about her money but more about the way Denny was acting. She confided to Ryan that Denny was not the same Denny she knew in college. Ryan said "ya I am not lost on that. He isn't even the same person that he was before we started the company". Becky stayed in the field and away from the plant for the most part and was just trying to put one foot in front of the other on what seemed like a death march for more investment money. Becky did stay busy including doing most of the patent work. Becky did have a law degree from Seattle University and did quality technical writing but with the new business model all the work had to be done again with regards to patents. Normal Norman was the only one walking around the headquarters with any kind of upbeat attitude. But even Normal Norman could sense the tenseness in the air. Norman envisioned rough sea's ahead for the company, especially in the short run. Even Norman could never have imagined how much of a physical and emotional toll the rough seas would have for everybody involved.

Chapter 2

Different Colored Ties

As with any small company capital, or the lack of it, is the number one reason for going out of business. Knowledge, or lack of it, is the second most likely suspect to having to close the doors at a company. "The Final Result" was now woefully undercapitalized and its knowledge base was at best in transition. Nerves and relationships everywhere in the organization were tense to say the least. Ryan and Denny had set out to help animals and make their mark on society in a positive way. Now everyone was stuck in what felt like a toilet bowl during flush mode. It seemed as though everybody was just swirling around in the work environment with their hands up. After almost a year the company still had no prototype that they could market or even demonstrate. Most of the prospective customers were either confused and or dismayed about the lack of follow through from the company and relationships where falling apart.

JD had several private communications with Chance Law to try to test the waters again about investment in the company. Surprisingly Chance was still really upbeat about the project if he could get a stake in the enterprise. Chance was even more intrigued by the new development of a no remote harness. In the first proposal Chance had always questioned the interaction of the owners operating the remote for the animal. He was convinced that this new harness had a much better chance to etch a notch in a new market. Even though JD was still hesitant to jump in bed with Chance he saw no alternative solution. JD called for a special board of directors meeting because he knew that he would have severe resistance from both Ryan and Terry that both knew Chances reputation. With all board members present he would at least have some individuals that could agree with his presentation.

The Monday morning meeting at 8am had an almost surreal feel to it for several board members. They felt like they were there physically, but it was almost like they were there just as an observer. Like a humming bird hovering over the conference table seeing and hearing everything that was going on, but not able to contribute. Not so for JD, he had brought his A game and dominated the entire four hour meeting. He outlined the bleak economic picture. Then he dropped the bombshell, "I see no other path to continue without an infusion of cash, and I see no other individual or group offering anything up except the possibility of Chance Law taking a majority share of the organization". The conversation stopped and everyone knew the future was not what they had all hoped it would be. JD situated himself mentally to defend his proposition. Instead he got relatively little reaction. Eileen chirped up and asked what Chance had already agreed to tentatively. Denny had said nothing and had not even been in the same room with Ryan for two weeks. Ryan finally capitulated and asked JD to lay out the details. Even with setting up the presentation, JD had many severely negative connotations about the plan going forward. Most of the other board members had anticipated how bad it was really going to be for everyone financially especially for JD and Eileen. JD explained that Chance was very savvy and could smell the blood in the water and was going to hammer out a hard deal to swallow. The bad news continued including a restructuring of the organization that would leave the following pecking order.

> Chance Law –Chief Executive Officer and Chairman of the Board-501 shares
>
> JD McGraw- President and Chief Operating Officer-139 shares
>
> Ryan Oxbow-Vice president of Marketing-120 shares
>
> Dennis Conner –Vice President of Research and Development - 120 shares
>
> Eileen House- Vice president of finance-120 shares

This distribution of more than 500 additional shares devalued previous shares by more than half. To say the least it was a bitter pill to swallow for the rest of the board members. The so called part time involvement would end for JD now and he would take the reins of the operation. The other board members were stunned. Denny was the most incensed even though JD and Eileen were the ones that would have their cash investment diluted. Ryan was just dismayed about everything, especially the loss of control of the company, which could devastate him.

From that point forward Denny would show he went entirely to the dark side. Denny thought after all this was his baby from the start and going from 25% share in the future to maybe 10% share was more than he was able to handle emotionally. After several more hours of mashing of teeth JD called for a vote. Denny stormed out of the meeting and yelled obscenities at JD as he was heading out the door. As it would turn out, it was to be Denny's last day of productive work for "The Final Result". The patents for the Harness where in Ryan and Denny's name but they had both long ago released the company to use the intellectual properties as it saw fit. Ryan and Eileen finally saw the finality of the situation and the final vote was 3 for, 1 abstains. The measure passed, but no one envisioned what would happen next. The two old corporate warriors JD and Chance had showed their fangs and dug in hard. Chance was offering up over 2 million in infusion of cash, and JD in charge of operations. At least the company was solvent again. But in the coming days that would be the least of everybody's worries.

Chance Law kept no office at "The Final Result" building and communicated strictly through JD. Over the next week JD grew the staff to 10 bringing on an additional accountant and some manufacturing techs as well as two administration assistants. Everyone was going through their paces and trying to get everything back on track. Denny was coming in just for a couple of hours in the morning and was just creating havoc when he was there. The meat of the final work on the harness had fallen to Doug. JD gave him a huge cash incentive to get the prototype harness operational by the end of the year-it was already late September. JD did not even counsel with Denny about the incentive to Doug. Denny went wacko about the bonus and now would be even more confrontational to everyone in the building during the week. So much so Ryan had to finally call the police to remove Denny from the premises on Friday. After the fiasco in the lobby with Denny and the police, including Denny actually being arrested and booked for disturbing the peace. Rumors on how that went down were flying through the building. It was Friday mid-day and JD sent everyone home for the weekend. Hopefully everyone would calm down and they could start again fresh Monday morning. That turned out to be anything but the truth. Denny posted bail and was out of custody by the end of the day.

Black Monday November 2nd came and the worst possible outcome began to unfold. The morning started normally and it appeared everyone was on board and at least attempting to go forward. Everyone except Denny and no one had even talked to him since Friday. He showed up just before ten AM and went directly to the machine floor. The machine floor was an open area 50 feet across and almost a 100 feet long. Two rows of production lines down the middle of the floor side by side separated from the middle by about 10 feet. Ten foot ceilings allowed for a raised three foot metal walk way with a four foot railing circling the entire floor so you could walk around the entire complex viewing it from any angle. After Denny entered the building he took his position mid floor on that raised walkway. Denny pulled from under his full length winter coat he wore, two double barrel shot guns and proceeded to open up on the production lines. Doug and his assistant dove for cover. Doug ended up with buckshot in his right shoulder but his assistant Steve caught a partial round in the neck and lay motionless on the cement floor. Doug caught a glimpse of Denny as he had turned reloaded and was walking toward the office area. Everyone in the building had heard the shots but they where muffled because the machine room had been insulated to almost a clean room environment. The outside environment of warehouses and low density manufacturing would leave no one from the outside calling for help, even if they did hear and recognize it was gun fire.

Somehow Doug was able to reach 911 on his cell phone and authorities where on the scene within two minutes with the knowledge that shots were fired and people where hit. Certainly the longest two minutes for everyone in the building. The first office down the hall from the machine floor was Terry Gwen's, Denny unloaded one round through the window of Terry's office door. Terry was under her desk unharmed but shaking violently from shock. She had not even seen who fired the shot. Denny continued down the hall reloading as he walked, it was clear that Terry, Doug and Steve were not high priority targets for Denny. The police still had Doug on the cell line but he was getting groggy from shock and his injuries so he was not much help tactically for the police.

Sergeant Harris a 29 year veteran on the police force made the split second decision to go in the front door of the office side of the building and try to cut off the assailant in the inside hallway before he could get to anymore offices. Sergeant Harris and officer Daveed went through the front door with vest on and weapons drawn. As they entered the building there was no one in the lobby and the entire building was eerily quiet. Everyone in the building had heard the shot from the hallway through Terry's office door and where scrambling to get out of their own offices. The next office used to be JD's that he used sparingly when he was just working part time and that Monday was the first Monday that Ryan had taken over that office space as JD had moved into Ryan's old office. That office door had a solid wood door and somehow Ryan had the presence of mind to lock it after he heard the gunshot outside Terry's office and before attempting to get out his little office window.

In the follow up investigation police determined that Denny probably thought it was still JD's office and he was the primary target after destroying the machine line he had set up for the product line. Denny unloaded on the wood office door but instead of aiming at the hinges or hardware he shot straight through the middle of the door. He even let go a second round from the other shotgun to the same area and the door amazingly still hung from the hinge and hardware sides. Just as Denny reloaded for the third time the police officers had made their way to the hallway and ordered Denny to drop the weapons and lay on the floor. Instead Denny ducked through the middle of Ryan's office door and then flipped and shoved the big wooded desk up to the door entrance. Ryan had scrabbled out the 12 inch by 30 inch swing open window and was hot footing it down the back alley and out of harm's way. JD would have never fit through that small window because physically he was a huge man standing six foot four and weighed well over three hundred pounds. By the time Denny peered out the window in Ryan's office all he saw was the swat team taking up positions in the alley.

At least the police now had Denny contained. The building was almost all cinder block and now all Denny had, was that small office window and the office front door as entry or exit points. Once the police knew they had him contained and had no hostages they were going to just stand pat until a negotiator was on site. Medical teams were now on site and were able to get to Doug and Steve on the machine room floor and get them out and on the way to the hospital. The swat team was now set up in the lobby area. JD and 4 other associates including Eileen where out of the building on the street. That group had thrown Ryan's old desk through the large plate glass window in Ryan's old office to escape. That window was the only large window in the entire building. The police now had Ryan, JD, Eileen, and Missy (JD's new assistant) in their safe custody and Doug and Steve on their way to the hospital. Chance Law and Becky had not been at the Building that Monday morning.

Ryan as he got his composure back and said "where the hell is Terry". Police were not able to move down the hallway yet as it was a shooting gallery from where Denny was held up. Once the police knew there was still one employee missing and possibly a hostage they moved down the hallway from the lobby toward the machine floor area. With 6 foot body shields now on site they moved down the hallway guarding them from any possible shots coming from Denny. They entered Terry's office and saw no one. Terry was still under her desk and was in total shock. She had wrapped herself in the fetal position and even with the help of officers she could not straighten out much less get on her feet. One of the larger officers on the swat team was finally able to get her hands unclasped and put her on his back and carried her out of the office and down the hallway and into the machine floor area. From there the medical teams were able to sedate Terry and get her on a gurney and off to the hospital. Terry had not said a word, and had a distant gaze in her eyes that were not even blinking even after sedation.

As the officers looked around the machine floor they saw Norman. He was cowering on a large shelf six feet above the machine room floor. Normal Norman was an 80 pound boxer that was almost 10 years old. He was wearing the latest version of the prototype harness. The police were amazed and talked amongst themselves asking each other, how the hell he got himself way up there. Several officers removed Norman from the shelf with the help of two ladders and reunited him with Eileen outside.

The negotiator was on site within an hour of the first shots. Bill Reams was a savvy veteran negotiator. Bill was a retired veteran sheriff of more than 20 years and now was just used as a private consultant by the local police force. Sarge, as he was known as at the police department took charge as soon as he was on scene. He was the closest of any of the other negotiating team members to the scene and parked his pick-up behind the police cars now on the steps of the building. Bill worked a plan to get a cell phone into the office Denny was in so he could attempt some communication with the power now shut off. Bill was small in stature but had a booming voice when he needed it. Through a blow horn Bill shouted down the hallway to Denny that he was going to shoot a blank gas canister through the small window that would contain a cell phone. He got no response from Denny. Bill ordered the shot and the canister went through the open window cleanly. Sarge kept calling the cell over and over with no response. Ryan had told Sarge that Denny did not have any close relatives and had lived on his own in a small apartment for several years. Denny did have one estranged step sister from a previous relationship that his mother had. She lived in Kentucky but no one had her full name much less a number to contact her. Beside's Denny had not talked to her in years so she would not be any help right then. Ryan mentioned Eileen knew him best next to him to Bill. Bill told Ryan to get her ready to talk to Denny over the megaphone. Just as Ryan was explaining the program to Eileen Denny finally answered the cell. The first words out of Denny's mouth were "are Doug and Steve OK?" Bill told Denny they were both stable and at the hospital. Bill had no idea what their conditions where but did not want Denny to believe he was now a murderer. Bill asked Denny "what exactly are you trying to do here?" After a long pause Denny said "Make JD pay". The cell phone went dead and everyone heard the self inflicted death shot. Bill gave the order to rush the office and there lay Denny with most of his head shot off by one of the shotguns. This was the last thing Ryan ever envisioned could happen. Norman looked at Eileen with such sad eye's she knew he understood what had just happened.

Chapter 3

How the Hell Did We Get to This

Everybody at the company was more than concerned, and the future of the company uncertain at best. Steve, through the miracle of modern medicine, was recovering but had a long journey ahead of him with skin graphs and other operations. Steve had been employed by the company less than a month. Doug was going to be OK too with therapy they said he should recover completely. Terry on the other hand was still traumatized and still had not uttered a word. Her family was holding strong at the hospital with all company employees dropping by to try to show their support. All of course except Chance Law, and nobody wanted to see Chance anyway.

The landscape had entirely changed including schisms between individuals that would last a lifetime. The company thank God had taken out key man insurance on all five principles Chance, JD, Ryan, Eileen and Denny, all at a million dollars each. This was common practice at the time for what was called highly compensated individuals in the insurance industry. In addition to that the company had a million dollar umbrella policy on accidents at the work site. Eileen and Becky with input from JD did a whale of a job having those policies in place at the time of the tragedy.

In another big turn of events, since Denny did not have any living family members except his step sister, he left all his earthly possessions to Ryan. Denny bequeathed this in a hand written plain will found in his apartment and properly notarized less than a year previously. Denny's will explained, that he had been shunned by his family even when the one's he knew where alive. Even his mother thought he was an interference with her pathetic life and showed

Denny very little love. The only real love Denny had ever got was from Ryan and his family. Denny ranted and raved though the document penned almost a year ago that he still had feelings for Eileen and his only true friend in the last decade was Ryan. Ryan had no idea that Denny had left him everything and he had no idea that Denny was so alone for so long. Ryan and Denny had extensive social activities over the last decade, but no other mutual friends. As Ryan began thinking back he could see now why all the friends and associates Ryan and Denny hung out with where introduced to Denny by Ryan. Ryan had seen Denny with very few girls and Denny often turned down offers from Ryan to get him set up with a date. Denny took his life at the age of thirty seven and left little else but the shares of stock in a company in shambles.

But oh what a gift those shares would turn out to be. Denny was not as good looking as Ryan, but held his own and more in a social atmosphere. However, nobody knew the dark side that Denny appeared to live in. The police investigation brought into the open that Denny had been involved in dark activities under anybody's radar. His office computer revieled nothing about how heavily involved he was with an association that actively participated in the occult. His home computer however showed Denny was heavily involved in the occult society in Portland that had ties to a national association. Investigator's fettered out that Denny had held a position of power within the group from Portland. However, they could not determine what position it might have been. Homicide detectives decided to turn what they found over to the special services department that had an ongoing investigation on the group. With the information they gained from the Denny investigators and what they already had on the group the special services investigators said they were ready to arrest other members of the same group on charges for sacrificing animals.

This issue turned out to be very awkward as you might think at Denny's services. Eileen brought Normal Norman to the services as she knew how close the two were after working daily with each other for over a year. Being the good judge of character that most dogs have Norman was agitated whenever he got close to the members of that dark occult association at the services. Everyone from the company turned out for Denny's services, except of course for Chance Law. Normal Norman in full harness was alert but had contained his composure and was respectful throughout the services. Ryan's parents were there with some of the other neighbors from his old neighborhood. Charles and Nona still could not get their brains around the idea that "their Denny" was in such a sad place. The occult connection was just vulgar to both Ryan's parents and neighbors. No one planned any gathering after the services. To add calamity to the services the media had caught wind of the occult issue and had cameras running when police officers arrested several people that where obviously with a group from the occult in the parking lot after the services.

JD had suspended operations for two weeks. Communicating through emails JD was able to schedule a board meeting Friday at the local Marriot before the target date of Monday December 3rd to resume operations. JD knew that continuing operations in the current building was going to be contentious at best and had talked with Chance and negotiated a deal to move operations to a more suburban location that was five miles away from the old building. Chance owned the new building and would lease the 30,000 square feet to the company at a much reduced rate for a year and with an additional year option.

Little did JD expect the meeting minutes to go the way they would. With only three members of the board present, Chance was once again absent. Ryan made his move. Neither JD nor Chance had any idea that Denny had left all his stock to Ryan which resulted in giving Ryan and Eileen majority voting rights for that meeting. With Eileen voting with Ryan the board passed a motion to put Ryan in as President and Chief Operating Officer and Chairman of the Board, Eileen as Chief Financial Officer, JD as vice president in charge of marketing, and Chance as vice president of investor relations. The tides had turned and Ryan with Eileen's help had almost wrestled control of the company back in to his hands. Ryan had hoped that because of the confusion around the death of Denny JD would not have gotten Chance's proxy to bring to the meeting. What JD and Chance did not see was Denny giving Ryan all his shares and they had one bigger gulp to still swallow.

With 499 shares controlled between Ryan, Eileen, and JD and 501 shares controlled by Chance it seemed like Chance still had control. But Ryan had one more card to play. In the next motion the board approved the new lease for the new building. In a final move Ryan introduce Brian Adams who was waiting in the lobby before Ryan called the front desk and asked him to come up. Brian was an old friend of Eileen's from Stanford that had a stellar resume that included software programming and start up money management. Brian was a geeky looking man with a pony tail, frail looking body, but with a monster mind for numbers. With Denny gone and Terry incapacitated Ryan knew he would need the kind of help Brian would bring, not to mention giving him the voting shares so Ryan would have ultimate control as long as he could get JD, Eileen, and Brian to vote with him in the future. The shares issued now stood at 1010, Chance had 501 and the rest of the board had 509. The board elected Brian as a board member with ten voting shares. The vote was two in favor one opposed. The take back was complete. JD was devastated and dreaded talking to Chance but subconsciously he thought it was great that Chance was no longer in control. Normal Norman attended the board meeting and was excited about the way it went. Thinking "Jesus, thank God Chance would have raped the place"

Chapter 4

The Negotiations

Chance Law was furious with JD at what had transpired. In the league Chance played in, control was all that mattered. Chance did not need the money, he did not need the work, and the only thing he knew he could not control was time. It would be the last time Chance would be so aloof at not attending board and corporate meetings of "The Final Result". It was the classic "too little to late" scenario. JD was no longer pinned in with Chance now and really started to like the present situation-hell it was a lot better than cow towing to Chance for the foreseeable future-a hell of a lot better. It would play out in the near term that JD would get back on board with Ryan and Eileen along with Brian to really drive the company forward. JD had never been a fan of Chance Law and now had the opportunity to operate independent of him and still have the funding needed to advance the product line. The company now was relatively well capitalized with Chance Law's infusion of cash as well as insurance payoffs. All major medical costs for Doug and Steve as well as counseling for all employees that felt they needed it, fell to another death and disability policy that was in place at the time of the tragedy. On top of that the company had a great lease for at least two years.

Because of the history in the old building Ryan contracted with a local moving company to move all items from the old building to the new location. The existing machine production line was about half destroyed as Denny knew which parts where expensive and or delicate. Ryan gave the moving company a deadline of a week to get everything moved. Ryan e-mailed everybody to be at the new building at 8am the following Monday morning for a new launch of company operations. Amazingly Doug was there and ready to get after it. Eileen was there with Normal Norman literally with bells on as it was less than a month till Christmas now. She had a new gleam on her face and it was not long before it was apparent that Ryan and Eileen had kindled their own sensual relationship during the dark time of the past several weeks.

JD was in the office and on the phone trying to restart conversations with past potential customers. He used the tragedy to excuse the lack of follow up and past guarantees of demonstrations. He really felt like a louse using it but had been through many corporate tragedies before and knew it was too valuable a tool to not use in order to get potential customers back on line. Brian was just trying to get his head around the company's finances and understand Terry's filing systems. Ryan got working with Doug to start to reassemble the production line and making lists of what they needed to order. Becky was working with Missy to align all the paper work that involved investments, loans, and grants to present to Chance.

The new building was in a relatively upbeat area with a bustling suburban environment and many services available in the local area. It would be a much easier environment in order to attract quality employees. Doug immediately tried to work with Norman and find out what triggered his ability to jump six feet in the air. If he could harness the chemistry that created the added lift to the harness he felt he could adjust the hardware to react to the endorphins and get a relative low adjustable scale that could be set and reset to an individual dog's needs and ability.

Ryan, Eileen and Doug worked together for an entire week on the issue and indeed were able to develop a chip placed just under the hide of the animal. It was the first time Normal Norman ever had to be sedated in order to facilitate a procedure. The implant would send demand information wireless to a tiny receiver on the harness and then on to the controller and vice versa. The controller actually worked well and had only three rudimentary settings for the owner/partner. Once Normal Norman came out of anesthesia and put on the harness, it was no more than a few minutes and he was wandering around the new production area with an unbelievable playful prancing gate. Norman was moving with relative ease and you could see he was moving with a very low level of pain, if there was pain at all. It was clear Norman had not felt this good in the year plus journey he had been on with the company. Ryan excitedly called Eileen and told her to get everyone down to the production floor. Nobody could believe what was going on and Eileen just started to cry and hugged Norman for a full minute taking in all the good emotions and relishing the thought of having Norman around for quite some time with a good quality of life.

Even Chance had happened to be in the building and was amazed at the demonstration. After a few minutes Ryan and JD where back at their desks setting up demonstration dates with prospective customers. Nobody envisioned what the breakthrough would bring. Except Norman, he understood how big that breakthrough was. Norman feared it was so big it would take on a life of its own and leave a wake of destruction in its path for all his closest friends. Norman also knew intuitively that the product would no doubt evolve even more.

Chance and JD separately had thoughts of the future that certainly where not the same as the other principles. Chance even had dark thoughts about how Ryan could meet with an accident. The money in the near future would be enormous and people and organizations often don't act with normalcy with that kind of money on the line. The next level of money would bring new pressure on the entire organization in ways that even Chance and JD would not be accustomed to.

Steve had come back to work which was a blessing for Doug and Eileen so Doug could continue with additional testing and let Eileen get back to the finance duties for the company. Steve and Ryan would team up to be the demonstration team along with of course Normal Norman. Norman was feeling as good as he had since he was half his age. JD would come along on demonstrations to hold the customer's hands, while Ryan, Steve and Norman would do the actual demonstrations. This also would allow Doug to stay on the production line. The company decided to lease a small jet aircraft called an eclipse. It was cramped for three people, the pilot and of course

Norman. They did not need much in the way of equipment so they could make it work. The contract was structured so the company could buy the plane when the lease ran out and all the lease payments would apply to the purchase price. With good scheduling and the need of only one pilot, Brian thought it was a prudent move. It would also allow the team to go out and back in many cases the same day to keep the accomodations costs down. With many of the potential customers being in California it would be reasonable to do those demonstrations in one long day. Norman liked the travel at first; in fact he relished the overnight stays because he would get pampered for the whole trip, rather than just go home with Eileen every night.

Eileen and Ryan had now bought a house together 15 minutes up the hill from the office. The house was a two story Tudor built in the 50's, very quaint and in terrific shape with mature landscaping. They moved in and Norman liked the 2 acre parcel the house sat on and had plenty to explore as at least an acre was heavily wooded. The entire parcel was totally fenced with six foot fences to keep the deer out. Eileen and Ryan could just let Norman out anytime and not worry about him mainly because the high fence kept the Coyotes out too. Norman would not stray off but had little chance with a pair of Coyotes. It was not long after buying the place Ryan put a doggy door in the back door so Norman could just come and go as he pleased. As the travel grind went on, Norman started liking only one or two extended days travel a month. Norman would wear down on long trips now and Ryan started to put a retirement schedule in effect in his mind for Norman. Eileen was also pushing to have Norman do a little less each day. Ryan and Eileen where both 38 years old now and where talking about having a baby. At that age the clock was certainly winding down for Eileen to have kids.

The staff at the company had grown to almost 20 people and the company was bustling along, but still had no firm customers. Chance's infusion of money was allowing the company to come back to life. The demonstration team had made 5 one day trips and 2 long distance demonstrations in Atlanta and New York. The cash situation was still OK at the company, but it would not be in a short time unless there were multiple revenue streams created. The latest trip initiated enough reaction that the large retail pet chain requested a follow up demonstration at "The Final Result" home office to inspect the production line. If Ryan, JD, and Chance had to choose from all the potential customers they would have picked the PK Company because it had the best potential to order and move large amounts of the product to the end users.

Bill Jones from PK enterprises and several associates flew in Monday. Chance and JD met them at the airport driving Ryan's company leased Suburban that JD now was driving. The group drove directly to the corporate head quarters in about 15 minutes. Ryan met them at the front door, and they all had coffee in the break room that doubled as the conference room. Ryan walked the group to the production area and everyone got seated for the follow up demonstration. Norman was to steal the show with the final act of demonstrating how he could literally jump onto a 4 by 4 foot stage four feet off the floor from a sitting position. Steve would then take the harness off and Ryan would try to encourage Norman to attempt that same jump and Norman would not even offer to bring his front paws up to the stage level. Bill was convinced, now the negotiations would start in earnest.

Chapter 5

More Negotiations

Ryan, JD and Chance sat down with Bill Jones and his team after the demonstration to discuss the specifics of a deal to carry the harness in their West Coast locations. Neither Ryan nor anybody else had any solid production schedule and had done little in the way of having a suggested retail price for the product. Brian had done some work on actual cost of production and they at least knew enough to throw a price out to Bill Jones. Bill was no novice in negotiations, however this product was so new compared to anything else they sold he had little idea what kind of price his customers would support. PK Company had 25 stores in the Western Region that included Washington, Oregon, California, Idaho, and Utah with 15 located in California. Distribution could easily be handled out of the current building because the company had not used all the square footage of the building with operations so far. By now the company had changed their doing business name from "Uplifting puppies" to "Harness Help". The company kept their original corporate name "The Final Result". The cost of production for parts and assembly alone was nearly 600 $ and Ryan had hoped they could wholesale it for somewhere north of 1,000 $ with a suggested retail price a little under 2,000 $. Ryan and Doug projected they could produce 50 harnesses a week comfortably with a monthly output of 200. That would give each location an inventory of 8 each for every store. They all went to lunch and agreed to leave everything on the table and start fresh in an afternoon session. Bill was sold on the product but was still unsure of its pricing marketability.

Bill met with his staff during lunch and decided to really push for a bottom feeder price. Given that the company was still a start up and had no other customers they started the afternoon session with an offer of 800 hundred dollars each expecting that they could retail it at 1,499.00. Ryan knew that was a very tight profit margin for the Harness but also could not just dismiss the offer. After all it was a huge offer that would bring in revenue of 160K a month and that may have just been the start of many more future orders. After some intense negotiations between Ryan and Bill separate from the group a deal was struck. The initial price to PK Company would be 850 dollars and PK would pick up the freight costs for all orders. PK's offer would also include paying for packaging costs per unit, including supplying SKU number decals, that would dovetail into PK's point of sale systems nicely. Ryan and Bill set the first ship date of product for March 1st. This would allow Doug to do the final testing and a month to gain adequate inventory in order to start actual shipments. So everybody thought.

The production line was adequate to punch out 200 harnesses a month but not many more. Terry was finally rehabilitated emotionally to come back to work part time and was helping Eileen set up the new distribution department. Eileen gave her an assistant that could do some rudimental tasks that Terry might need, but was primarily employed to be Terry's body guard while she was at work and secondarily responsible for overall building security. Terry was still not stable enough emotionally to work at her desk without other people around. She of course was compensated with her normal salary along with covering all the psychological treatments while she was out of commission. Ryan scheduled yet another board meeting when he knew Terry was coming back. The main reason was to discuss and issue Terry some stock as she should be compensated additionally for her emotional distress. Terry had helped the company get off the ground and paid a dear price for just being employed by the Company. She could have taken the whole episode another direction and see if she could file suit and get a huge settlement. Fortunately, Terry held no bad feelings against Ryan or anybody else. On the contrary she wanted to get back to work and get some more normality back in her life. She had never really thought about settling and never had the money greed problem. Terry was awarded 20 voting shares and that would bring her back into the decision making for the Company, which is what she wanted.

The board also passed a motion to elect Becky Germane to the board with no voting shares. This would bring the board to seven members and that was a comfortable level for quorums, knowledge, and diversity. Terry was female and was originally from Australia and Becky was female, black and was raised in Alabama. JD was originally from New York and still had a house there that his ex-wife lived in. JD was the prototype male white executive that was fairly uncoordinated and uncomfortable with his size. With Brian, Ryan and Eileen being white and from the West Coast the board was pretty well rounded. The motions passed 4 to 1 with Chance voting no on both measures.

It was now very clear Chance was now isolated and was playing as the "wild card player on the board". Before he ended the meeting Ryan had instructed all board members to think about the expansion to double what they currently had. He directed Eileen, Brian and Terry to meet during the next month and bring a presentation back to the board with recommendations on cost and how to move forward. No one was lost on the fact that no matter what the plan, the company would need even more additional capital. With some good news Becky brought up that she had acquired a grant from PETA that had no strings attached in the amount of 100,000. Once again Becky showed them how to find grant money. Normal Norman was pretty comfortable throughout the meeting on his newly installed pedestal that sat him at the opposite end of the conference table from Ryan and allowed him to be at eye level with all the other people at the table, he thought it was a very prestigious position. Eileen always sat to Norman's right so she could easily stretch out her hand in a seated position and still pet Norman's head.

Chapter 6

The Procedure Goes Away
(unimaginable timing)

The first Monday morning in February was cold with freezing rain that made everybody late. At 9 am Doug and Brian stopped by Ryan's office and asked him if he had a half hour or so to listen to some testing developments. Brian and Doug had been working weekends on a project that neither Ryan nor anybody else knew about. Ryan was free till 10 and invited them into his office. Brian explained that they had been working secretly on a chip that was attached to a collar that could pick up the same information that the chip that had to be imbedded in the animal. Ryan and JD had been having issues with other prospective customers because they were not capable of doing the procedure or were at least concerned about the extra cost of the procedure. PK Company was able to handle the procedure because they had quality staff at each store that could do the procedure without much cost.

Ryan asked about the difference in cost for the two chips. His jaw dropped when they said it would be half the cost along with no cost for any procedure. He asked JD to come down to his office and JD responded that he had a full schedule all day and could they meet Tuesday morning. Ryan told him to clear an hour and get down to his office now. JD was miffed when he came through the door hitting his head on the low door jamb as he did almost every time he entered Ryan's office, but was soon listening intently to what Brian was explaining. After he got his thoughts together JD asked how long until they could have it fully tested and start manufacturing? Doug said at least six weeks. JD turned to Ryan and said "did you forget we have contracts signed with delivery scheduled in 45 days!" Ryan told him to settle down and asked Brian and Doug to go back to work and keep quiet about this and scheduled to have lunch with them at noon.

Ryan immediately got a call into Bill at PK and asked for an emergency meeting and told him they could fly down this afternoon and meet in their offices bright and early Tuesday morning. Bill said fine. JD and Ryan both knew they had to delay the launch and get the new product to PK instead of the old imbedded chip harness. JD and Ryan had lunch with Doug and Brian. It became clear to Ryan that the new development was already well on its way to being the standard for the company. Missy had ordered sandwiches in and the group ate in JD's office. As lunch ended Ryan told JD and Brian to be at the plane by 3 pm. JD said "hey nobody even had a change of clothing or toiletries". Ryan said gather up the information we need for the meeting and get to the plane. He then asked Missy to run to the nearby men's boutique and get a change of clothes for all of them and stop at Walgreens and get toiletries for all of them. Ryan booked them all into the nearby Marriott in San Francisco next to PK Enterprises. He then sent a mass e-mail to all employees' now numbering 25, explaining briefly the new development.

Norman was willing to go as he had yet again been the test dog for the new chip without Ryan or Eileen's knowledge. Eileen popped into Ryan's office before he left and told Ryan he needed to sit down. Ryan's mind was racing and was annoyed that Eileen was not just excited and offering to help him get ready to travel. He then got an even bigger bomb laid on him than Brian and Doug had given him first thing this morning. She explained that she had a doctor's appointment this morning and the doctor had confirmed she was pregnant. He was stunned to say the least but immediately grabbed her and swung her around in his arms. It was now almost 2pm and for the next hour he locked his office door and made mad crazy sex with Eileen. He could have put the trip off a day but he thought it through and the team was in the air headed South by 3:30 pm.

Ryan, JD, and Brian met at the Marriott till about 10pm and were settled enough to decide to get a good night's sleep and be fresh for the 8am meeting. As he lay there in his hotel room trying to go to sleep Ryan's mind was still racing about all that had happened to him in one single day. The room looked just like every other hotel room in the country to Ryan and he was getting tired of traveling. Ryan's primary thoughts were concentrated on Eileen and the new baby growing inside her. However, he could not get out of his head how much had gone on at the company in the last six months. The death of a friend, that in the end he never even really knew and the growth of a company that started with just an idea. How and why was he so lucky? How did Denny's life go so awry? He always knew he had the ability to organize people and get them to do what he wanted them to do without telling them to "Do It". Ryan vowed himself to protect his back as he knew the future would bring even more twists and turns that he would have to deal with. Trust no one he told himself as he started to drift off to sleep.

Norman whimpered at him from the floor and he got up and helped Norman onto the bed. At night and before long naps it was best to remove his harness to avoid what basically were bed sores. Ryan then took the over the counter sleeping pill that Missy had the good sense enough to have in each toiletry pack. He set his alarm on his cell phone and laid down next to Norman-All was well with the world Ryan thought. Ryan woke up at 3am, jumped up to a sitting position and said "OH SHIT". In his haste he had told Eileen that he loved her like crazy. He had not done her the honor of asking her to marry him. He tossed and turned the rest of the night and was out running on the street by 6am to try to get some of the anxiety out of his body. Norman thought Ryan was so over analyzing everything that had happened the day before and was concerned that he would not be on top of his game for the meeting in 2 hours. Norman was also a little put out that he had his own sleep interrupted. Everybody was excited and anxious including Norman about the meeting at 8am. Ryan always tried to get in a run early in the morning around 6am. It was no different today he ran for about half an hour around and around the hotel complex at a brisk pace to try to reduce his anxiety over the upcoming meeting. Norman slept in that day as Ryan ran.

The team had breakfast at 7am at the restaurant across the lobby in the Marriot. Ryan had got used to presenting Norman as a guide dog and would bring him to the table without asking anybody if it was OK. Many times in the past he would ask but they would often time's say no. So Ryan just used the "assumed close" and placed him at his feet at the table. Nobody ever said much because they would see the harness and Norman would play it up to the hilt, even to the point of sometimes growling at anybody that would bring up that dogs were not allowed in here. After all Norman did not want to be back in the room alone and there was never any table scraps in the room.

Bill welcomed the group at the headquarters front door. The group exited the taxi from the short six block ride and looked up at the massive 3 story building on a bluff with full view of the San Francisco Bay. Bill had no idea of the specifics and was anxious as well. They met in the decadent boardroom of PK Enterprises that had a mauve color scheme and expensive art all around the room. It was very intimidating for Brian and even a little for Ryan. Neither had ever really been invited to a high end board room like this one. You could have been in a large legal firm's conference room in New York. JD on the other hand took the environment in stride as he had seen too many of these type rooms over the years.

Norman just thought it was sterile and might even have a little scent of evil. Although that scent was one of the few times Norman got his wires crossed. JD made the presentation and explained for an hour the benefits of the new collar chip and how it would be so much more customer friendly. JD was very smooth in his presentation including telling them that even though the new chip was most likely a little more in cost than the embedded one "The Final Result" would honor the contract price of the original harness. JD went on to say that in good conscious the company had to come clean with PK company about the new development even though they had a signed contract for the old product. By now JD even had conservative Bill thinking wow this is great and all we have to do is delay the sales launch by a month or two.

Ryan and JD had discussed this strategy the previous day and both decided to have JD pitch it this way thinking that Bill and PK would likely try to beat them down on price. They did have a fallback position to reduce the cost of each unit due to production delays. JD even thought they might be in trouble and feared PK could sue for not fulfilling contract obligations. JD finished the presentation and Ryan, Brian and Norman did an abbreviated demonstration as the new chip did basically the same thing as the old chip did without human involvement. Norman was glad to do the demonstration as he was tired of hearing the bullshit that JD was spewing.

After the demonstration concluded Bill recommended that the group have a tour of the PK distribution complex and he would meet back up with them for lunch. Bob the GM for the PK distribution center came in and walked the group through a quadrangle park like area; it was an open air green space in the middle of the complex, over to the distribution center. Bob was short, chubby and bald with a bushy mustache. Brian was enthralled with the distribution operation and was trying to take it all in. Ryan and JD where walking together separated by yards from the main group discussing options under their breaths.

At noon Brian asked Ryan if he could stay a while at the distribution center while JD and Ryan went to lunch with Bill. Bob said they would just order in some sandwiches and eat with the work force in the lunch room. Brian had questions about the operations and he could use the knowledge he could gain on the "The Final Result" company's new distribution center. Ryan said great and he and JD went back over to PK headquarters to meet up with Bill for lunch. Norman stayed with Brian because he thought he could get more table scraps from the lunch room crew at the distribution center.

Bill greeted Ryan and JD in the lobby, obviously the GM had given him a heads up that Ryan and JD where coming back. Bill was standing with a mountain of a man that even dwarfed JD's mammoth size. Neither Ryan nor JD had ever seen him before. His name was Perry Hickle and he was founder and CEO of PK Enterprises. He had started the company 20 years ago with one store when they were located in Salt Lake City. Perry had built the company into a 2 billion dollar power house. Perry and Bill had talked the situation over and had a counter proposal that would blow Ryan and JD away.

After the introductions Bill said we have a car waiting on us out front. They all piled into a Mercedes SUV and where off to Perry's favorite lunch spot. Vancouver's restaurant was on the water and had the typical steak and seafood fare. The group got a window table that looked out at the marina and was in a small room removed from the main floor of the restaurant. The restaurant manager sat them and asked if anyone else besides Perry wanted a drink before lunch. JD asked Perry what he was having, and Perry said he always has at least one long island tea before he had his lobster tails. Ryan and JD both said they would join him and Bill ordered ice tea.

The group all sat and chatted with drinks about the situation and Perry looked at JD and said "This is what I propose" "We will throw out the old contract and start fresh with the new product and new contract". Perry explained how he had a similar issue a decade ago with a different product. That company did not disclose that they had an enhanced product coming up and just sold the old product to PK Enterprises. That company even sold the new product to other competitors. Perry would never forget that, and was impressed that a startup company had the guts to put a promising 2 million dollar yearly revenue steam on the line and be honest about it. Anyway he said, he would delay the sales launch till May 1st and keep the same order and price on the new product. He also said PK would order an additional 200 harnesses in the fall. Perry then blew everybody's socks off including Bill. Perry said "I might even consider investing in "The Final Result" in order to get the infrastructure for the expansion on a fast track." JD and Ryan had no idea that Perry had crossed paths with Chance Law in the past and had a huge grudge against him-but Bill did.

Ryan kept looking at his drink and thought am I drunk or is this guy really saying this stuff. JD kept his composure and said we could agree in principle on the new contract and additional order. JD said that any new contract would be pending a vote by the board of directors. JD then asked how long before the board at PK enterprises could get a legal agreement in writing to them? JD was hoping that he could bide some time to think this all out. Perry looked at JD smiled and said "I am the board and the documents will be ready for you to take back this afternoon." They all had lobster tails and another long island tea, except Bill all he had was a continuous flow of ice tea. Turns out, Bill was Perry's brother in law and was a Mormon. Bill and Perry were at the opposite end of the spectrum in about every other issue except work. It was clear Perry valued Bill's input but Perry was the real power house behind the operation. Ryan told Perry he would also take up the investment issue with the board. They returned to PK headquarters and gathered up Brian and Norman along with the documents and where back at the airport headed home by 3pm.

JD sat down in the jet and looked at Ryan and said "God Dam it-we have nearly 4 million dollars on the line and all we really have is a fricken prototype". This was the end of the embedded chip and the procedure that went along with it. Norman would be the only dog to ever have had it imbedded.

Chapter 7

The Cats Claws Begin to Show

Ryan once again called for a board meeting for Friday morning. Chance was there along with all board members. The discussion for approving the new PK contract including the additional 200 harnesses in September was short because no one saw a down side that was bad enough to not move forward. The risk of course was that the company would not be able to gear up fast enough to be able to support the September order. Brian said he and Doug where confident they could have the first 200 harnesses produced by mid April in order to allow the first months order to be on time to PK enterprises. Terry said she was confident 7 to 10 days was doable to get the freight to the destinations.

Eileen had run some preliminary numbers on cost of renovation and gear up and the number was staggering to the small company. She told everyone we are going to have to give up a lot of the company to attract that kind of money. She explained that there was even a smaller number of investment groups and or individuals that would play at that level. When you talk about millions of dollars you have a certain limited amount of players that are somewhat competitive. Above that level there are even fewer people or groups that have that kind of money and be willing to take the risk on a product that had not delivered even one unit and had no sales history. The company may never get to the 100 million dollar table but for affect she told the board that there were only 6 or 7 places to go for that kind of money.

Chance stood up and decided to hold school and explain that there was plenty of cash to go after in the arena that they were about to play in. Chance said Eileen hit it on the nose, how much value of the company are they willing to give up and or how much interest they could palate. Chance even said he could find the money but it would be north of 8% interest. "The Final Result" had exhausted the governmental loans and grants and any of the banks they had dealt with were at their cap on credit for the company. The board agreed to let Chance bring back his best offer and the board would meet again a week from Monday.

Ryan and JD had not mentioned Perry's offer to invest to the rest of the board except For Eileen. Norman seemed bored with all this money stuff and napped through much of the meeting. Eileen said she had two final issues for the board to take up today. She said they needed to get someone into a customer relations position because she had been fielding an increasing number of general inquisitive calls about the product. Ryan nominated Missy and the board agreed to offer her the manager position for customer service. She had a great ability to communicate especially with people that where on edge.

Eileen also said she thought the company should make Terry vice president for distribution so she could back off from her accounting duties and she could start the development of the company's web site which had virtually no work done on it. Ryan and the board agreed but also gave Eileen the additional position of vice president of media relations. Eileen would now be Missy's boss so she could kick any sticky situations up to Eileen. Some crazy lady had been calling about abuse claims that the harness was prejudice against cats and demanding that they produce a sister product that would be able to help cats. Eileen did not want anyone but her to handle this kind of inquiry because there is not a good solution to these kinds of issues. Eileen wanted to have Missy handle the calls that wanted legitimate information and leave the wacko's for her to deal with. Some people just have to be placated and hope that eventually they just fade away. Norman got a chuckle out of that thinking to himself "when was the last time you saw a cat that had bad hips".

JD followed Ryan back to his office to discuss the Perry deal in seclusion. Of course, he was reading some correspondence and bumped his head again on Ryan's office door jam. JD told Ryan "get somebody in to raise this blasted header on your office door". Ryan got on the phone and called Perry's cell and to his surprise he answered it on the second ring. Ryan explained that the company was looking in several different directions for expansion funding and wanted to know what Perry was interested in offering. Even JD was surprised when Perry said he would be willing to go either way. He offered near 6% loan money that was unheard in the commercial environment or he would invest the 2 million that it would cost to expand and take controlling interest in the operation. After some more conversation Ryan told Perry he would get back in touch with him early next week after he and his team crunched more numbers. Perry said great he would look forward to hearing from him-he then told Ryan to say hi to JD as he knew he was listening.

Chance requested a sit down with Eileen, Ryan and JD at the end of the week to discuss what options he was able to round up as far as seed money. Chance had two real options. The first was from a Wall Street investment firm that had plenty of cash on the sidelines waiting for a hot product. The other was with an undisclosed individual investor. Both where loan propositions with interests at 8.5 percent. The individual investor was more than likely Chance himself. Ryan asked if he had floated any trial balloons in the way of investment for a share of the company to any potential investors. Chance said sure but there was very little interest and it would take additional time to get prospective investors through the process of explaining the new business model. Ryan told Chance to keep pursuing options and they would meet again later next week.

Ryan reflected over a long weekend getaway with Eileen and Norman on how to proceed. They went to a favorite get away of theirs on the Oregon Coast. They had been there several times way before they were a couple. Denny, Ryan and Eileen all loved the coast, especially this little motel. The drive was only a little over an hour and winter on the Oregon coast city of Seaside was quaint with monster rain and wind storms. They always stayed at the little "Apple motel" that was on the sand and had a restaurant and bar attached to the same building. The bar had a huge fire place with a view of the Pacific

Ocean that was breathtaking. Eileen, Ryan and Norman could walk the beach and return to the motel for hot food and drinks. Jeff Stills owned the motel and the bar and grill and for years now had gotten to know Ryan, Eileen and especially Norman. Jeff had even attended Denny's service. Norman was not only allowed in the lounge but usually sat where Jeff was even if he was not sitting with Ryan and or Eileen. Norman and Jeff would often times go for walks without Eileen or Ryan. Norman loved the coast and thought on several occasions that he could smell the scents of the Orient from the ocean surf. Jeff thought hey, they find glass bottles from the Orient washing up all the time. Jeff was one of the few people that Norman ever bonded to hard besides Eileen and Ryan and they had a joint spirit that was evident to anybody. As the years went by Ryan and Eileen saw Jeff have this kind of relationship with many other dogs. Jeff for some reason never had a dog, but there was almost always at least one dog at the inn. Not once had Ryan or Eileen seen a dog confront another dog at the inn. Jeff seemed to create a safe environment for them and they respected his territory. Ryan asked Jeff one day why he did not have a dog himself. Jeff responded by saying he just could not deal with losing a dog again. Jeff did have a dog before Ryan knew him and he had lost him in a freak surf accident and Jeff never really got over the episode.

Ryan walked and walked the beach in search of answers but in his heart he knew he could never trust Chance nor would Chance ever trust him. This dynamic had to stop as it was a going to only get worse. Besides it was fairly evident that Perry would come in with the best deal. JD stayed at the office most of the weekend crunching numbers with Brian. Ryan had shared with Brian what was going on with Perry and asked him to work with JD over the weekend. Brian was not excited about creating additional debt, but the offer of 6% loan money he thought was obviously the best deal. With the improved profit margin on the new chip he thought the company would have the ability to pay this down in the short term.

After meeting with JD and Brian on Monday morning they were all convinced that the Perry deal was what they needed to pursue. JD and Ryan now knew any offer from Chance or Wall Street now were one in the same. Wall Street people do not have a heart and it's all about the money and only the money. With the Perry deal at least they still had control and added an investment partner that has a thematic connection and a vested interest in the success of the product. Perry hoped secretly that the company would default and he could call the loan and take control of the company. This might have been the evil Norman picked up on earlier. Ryan, JD and Brian where headed back to San Francisco on the jet Tuesday morning early to meet again with Perry. This was going way out on the edge for everybody on "The Final Result" team. The potential was extreme, but so was the risk. Norman was bored because he did not have a lot to do. The entire rest of the team was focused on the production of the first 200 harnesses. He just wandered around the headquarters' and visited everybody throughout the building. Norman had when people ate lunch and where, down to a science.

Perry picked up the team at the executive field business office at the Airport in his hummer and drove them all out to his palatial mansion overlooking San Francisco bay. The place made the decadent PK boardroom look like a paupers lounge. The home had huge spacious area's spread out in every direction. It was a nice day so Perry had them set up on the veranda overlooking the Olympic size pool and huge spa tub to go over the details. The pools far side was made of glass and it gave the illusion that the pool water went straight out to the bay waters in the distance.

Bill had already seated himself at the table and stood up to greet them as they sat down. Perry asked everyone if they would like something to drink. At that point the butler appeared at the table waiting to take orders in a sharp as a tack conventional butler outfit. Even though nobody at the table was brought up in low end environment this was simply over the top, at least for Ryan and Brian. Perry said he would have his usual and everybody else said they would join him. Bill said ice tea-no sugar. It was eleven o'clock in the morning when the butler returned to the table with four huge glasses of long island tea and Bill's ice tea in a corny little amber goblet.

Ryan asked if this offer was completely separate from any contract they currently had with PK Enterprises. He was a little surprised to see Bill at Perry's house involved in a separate investment. Perry explained that yes it would be a completely separate agreement and Bill was also his private attorney as well as a principle at PK Enterprises. After several hours of conversation and two rounds of drinks they had a rough general agreement that Bill would clean up legally and have something for Ryan to bring back to the board for ratification this afternoon. Bill then excused himself as the butler re-appeared and said lunch is served. He escorted the group into a huge dining room that could have sat 20 people comfortably. They had a medley of lobster, shrimp and clams. After lunch Perry invited the group to go down to the marina and take a short cruise on his boat around the bay.

They all boarded what had to be a fifty foot yacht with a crew of two and they were off for an afternoon of sunny skies and calm seas. Ryan thought if Chance knew what they were doing and where they were doing it his hair would be on fire. Brian was just in awe and Ryan was worried this was way too good to be true. JD and Perry where telling old corporate war stories and now where getting pretty well ripped. The first mate had made a pitcher of a rum concoction and continually kept filling up everybody's glasses. The captain asked Perry what he wanted to do. Perry said, "it's so nice out let's take a run out to the ocean." After the no-wake zone the captain opened up the dual 8 cylinder engines full bore and they were flying out of the harbor. By the time they all got back to the marina Ryan and Brian where woozy and JD and Perry where drunk. Perry instructed the driver to take us to the airport and he was going to stay at the marina until he was able to return and pick him up. Ryan said what about the legal documents. Perry squawked back that Bill had already dropped them off at the airport with your pilot. "The Final Result" jet had wheels up by 5pm on its way back north. Everybody slept in the air and felt like crap as they landed. The team was not use to partying and traveling for business at the same time.

Wednesday morning Ryan called for a full board meeting Friday at 8am. Chance of course thought it was going to be his presentation that would take center stage. Chance knew JD and Ryan had something cooking but he did not expect them to have signed documents that would move the operation forward let alone at discounted rates. As the meeting was called to order Chance was struggling with paperwork to make sure he was ready for his presentation. Ryan presented the offer from Perry in a short curt manner and then turned to Chance and asked if he had any other option that could compete. Of course he knew he did not. Chance got extremely red faced and slammed his file folders on the table and shouted "why the hell am I doing all this work if you never intended to use or even listen to any of my proposals". JD said they needed to explore all options, and if he had something they should explore further they would listen. Chance knew he was screwed, and stormed out of the meeting. Ryan asked Brian to go after him and try to get him calmed down and come back to the meeting. Ryan adjourned the meeting and rescheduled a restart at 1pm. hoping that would allow Chance time to calm down. Norman thought "Jesus how can Chance be such an ass hole-he doesn't even like dogs"

Brian caught up with Chance and got him to agree to go to an early lunch with him. Chance did not know what to do so he agreed to get the hell out of the building and have something to eat. Brian excused himself briefly from Chance and told him he would meet back with him in the lobby in ten minutes. While Brian picked up his coat in his office he called Ryan and told him he would do his best to get Chance back to the board room by 1pm. Ryan was relieved, considering what happened the last time somebody stormed out of a board meeting. Ryan told Brian to stick with Chance till then and if he needed anything to call him on his cell.

During lunch with Brian Chance was still mad as hell and even asked Brian what he would take for his shares in the company. He was still mad enough that he was trying to figure out if he could somehow buy all the existing loans the company had, and along with his shares try to pressure the rest of the board to vote for a takeover by him or a combination of him and other outside investors. He finally did calm down and came to grips that Ryan and JD had more than enough strength to withstand any challenge he could currently bring. Chance was so arrogant that he did not even remember he had burned Perry on a deal 15 years ago when he was a principle in an investment group in New York that turned down Perry's first attempt at an IPO when PK Enterprises was just starting to try to go public. Perry was able to eventually launch PK Enterprises into a public company creating a huge infusion of money that allowed PK vast rapid expansion. After paying some huge salaries and huge bonuses to himself and other family members for years, Perry was able to smoothly buy back shares of the company. Perry and several family members now held more than 60% of the company and had for a number of years. Perry was the only one that even remembered or knew about the past issue with Chance and there was no doubt the real reason he had offered his investment at such a low return.

Ryan brought the meeting back to order shortly after 1pm and the motion to accept and sign the loan contract passed 6 to 1. Chance resigned his position at the company that afternoon and told Ryan all future communication involving his shares of the company would now need to be through his lawyer in Washington DC. His private lawyer was a partner in one of the best takeover firms in the world. Ryan wished him the best and told himself "The wolf is always at the door". Chance also resigned as a board member. Ryan would have to now worry about Chance over his shoulder and keep his guard up. Norman thought "good riddance"

Chapter 8

The Bureaucrats Run for Cover

Ryan began to research legal help and wanted to bring on a lead council for the company, as many legal issues needed attention and neither he nor JD would be able to keep up with them. He also knew that any communication with Chance's lawyer would have to now go through his own attorney. Becky did have a law degree from Seattle University but she had her hands full now, without help and support from Chance and would have to now take on all investor relations herself. JD thought he had the perfect match. He introduced Ryan to a long time friend Chuck Hikel that he had sent the plane to Los Angeles to pick up. Chuck had a business degree from Harvard and a law degree from Stanford. He had been consulting for a large law firm in L.A. after a 20 year stint with a Washington D.C. law firm. He retired as a partner from that firm five years ago and at the age of 52 was looking for what he could do for the next 5 to 10 years that would challenge him. "The Final Result" could not match his past compensation but Ryan was willing to give up some small interest in shares to him. He had all the money he really needed and he wanted to get passionate again about the work he was doing. Besides he loved the Northwest and wanted out of California. JD, Ryan and Chuck agreed in principle to have Chuck installed at a six figure salary as General Counsel for" The Final Result" pending board approval. He would also be awarded 20 shares of common stock as a signing bonus and take a position as a board member.

Doug had been elevated to Director of Research and development. Steve now had the title of Director of Engineering and now had people with mechanical engineering degree's working for him. Steve had no formal training as an engineer but could out think anybody mechanically. He knew the production line and all its components better than maybe even Doug. The total team at headquarters now numbered in the 30's and things were getting pretty exciting as the deadline was approaching where the company would actually deliver their first order.

Ryan with urging from Eileen decided to hold a launch party the Saturday after the May 1st deadline. Missy was put in charge of getting invitations out to all employee's and family, vendors, friends, local bankers, and even some local dignitaries including a city council member, that lived in the district where the company was located. JD told her to make sure she sent an invite to all potential customers too. Missy had now grown into a kind of Chief of Staff for Ryan and had hired several other people to field customer service inquires. She was invaluable to the office team and really was taking charge of everyday activates. She even mentioned to Ryan that he should offer to have the plane go down and get Perry for the party and take him home Sunday. What a great idea, Ryan said, and directed her to make that happen.

Perry was so excited he called Ryan himself after he got his special invitation and told him he would not miss the event. Perry had rented private aircraft for himself in the past but no one had ever sent their plane for him. Ryan asked Perry if he was going to bring Bill along. Perry said Bill adds little or nothing to a party scene. He said he would bring along his private assistant that would be able to handle Perry's private needs. As it turns out he would bring the same butler guy along dressed in impeccable 70,s attire as Missy had made the launch party a throwback disco theme to ramp up the energy. The Launch party was schedule in the ballroom at the Marriot down the street from Headquarters at 7pm.

Everyone at the office was working crazy hours because it was now the first week in April and Brian's self imposed Date of the 15th of April to have 200 harnesses ready to ship was approaching fast. Steve kept the line staff 2 hours extra overtime every weekday. He would help Doug when he could on the new production line that was being built and would double the capacity of production of harnesses by the middle of

August. More power would be needed and Doug had brought in a local electrical contractor to make the electric capacity of the building to 3 phase service. Ryan had told Doug to just do it and don't worry about turning the cost over to the building's owner. He wanted him to alert the commercial marketing firm that managed several buildings for Chance or one of his companies about the upgrade and explain to them the cost of the upgrade would be absorbed by "The Final Result". Ryan feared that Chance would block or slow the upgrade down if he found out they needed it that badly just for sour grapes. Chance certainly was capable of this, even though he still had a vested economic interest in seeing the company grow and expand.

In another weird turn of events, the contractor that was doing the upgrade had an electrician that was working on the project jump off the roof and kill himself. He had been in the rafters setting conduit and found the roof access hatch and literally just walked off the roof in the middle of the day. At first everyone thought it was an accident. The police said they would do an investigation and determined that no one else was involved in the incident. That was late Tuesday, and by Wednesday noon the company had several investigation units on site doing their investigations and also had an OSHA representative wandering around the machine floor asking Steve questions about the safety features of the manufacturing line.

All this activity was holding up a normal production day with less than a week till the deadline. Even though everybody was upset at what had happened they were all trying to keep their nose to the grindstone knowing what was on the line. Ryan determined the chaos was not productive so he sent everybody but the office staff home for the day. Ryan also told everybody to take Thursday off and return on Friday morning for work. For rest of the day Wednesday and for most of Thursday Ryan and Doug worked with the local and state police. They also dealt with the OSHA representative to iron out any issue's they had on any front. The police had gone through the electrician's apartment and found a suicide note detailing that he was distraught about a recent separation from his wife. She had filed for a restraining order against him for herself and her five children. He was also under pressure from a domestic violence violation and was due in court Friday morning for sentencing. Somehow his employer was unaware of his situation and continued to send him out on jobs. That one item took the investigations away from any future investigation of company operations. In the end the death was determined to be suicide.

Norman often times was found outside sitting at the spot where the man landed with a sad look on his face. Norman could sense death over the years and found it comforting to gaze off into the distance at spots where something, even an animal had died. Eileen often talked about this anomaly with Norman because she had seen it so many times. She often told Ryan that he was showing respect for the dead. Norman himself made the analogy to the living human world, they should show respect for each other. Even in the wild, animals respect each other and kill only for their own sustainability. In the corporate world you get the same answer, people think they have to kill or command in order to advance and further sustain themselves and their families. Norman still often thought "Man, why can't they all understand that you get more from respecting others, every time." He also kept thinking "you can't expect respect from anybody if you don't give it up first". Besides in the corporate world you should show it because you never know who will be working for whom down the road. Norman was about to witness how well demanding respect works out for a complete bureaucrat.

The OSHA representative was still pontificating on the machine floor about this and that and how this or that may not be in compliance. Ryan had called Chuck down to meet with this crazy inspector that was not even there for an inspection of the company operations. After the representative was done with his tirade Chuck invited him into Ryan's office and asked for his card. Chuck then called his office and asked for his supervisor. The representative got very agitated and said I think we can just issue a warning and have you change a few things and have me come back in 30 days to re-inspect. Chuck and Ryan thanked him and escorted him to the door. Timing is everything, if the production line was shut down; there was no way they could have met the production schedule. It was a lesson relearned for Ryan to avoid bureaucrats at all costs. Norman had hung around because Eileen was still working and he was having a ball with the other investigators. Doug and Norman were demonstrating how the harness worked to the investigators. Norman ignored the OSHA representative even when he tried to lure him over with his favorite dog bones that were spread out all over the machine floor so anybody could easily give him a treat. This was yet another testament to Norman's good judgment of character in people.

Chapter 9

Sometimes good people get thrown under the Bus
(But nearly every time they are at least complicit in the crime)

Bill from PK and Brian from The Final Result communicated for each company in preparation of the sales launch May 1st. Brian had started to get full of himself and started isolating Steve from Doug and running his plays with Bill at PK without authorizing them with Ryan. Brian thought that he was now irreplaceable and such a value to the company that he should make decisions that formerly he would have never made by himself. Steve and Brian had become close over the last several months and even socially met at some of the local gay bars in downtown Portland. Ryan had got wind of the relationship from Eileen because she was always at the office and would see them arrive at work together, go to lunch together, and most of the time leave together. Ryan told her they should mind their own business as long as it was not having a negative impact on the company.

The storm clouds started to form after JD had briefly talked to Perry and he had mentioned some logistical decisions that Brian and Bill had made. JD went to Ryan to ask him why he had not mentioned these to him. Of course JD banged his head on Ryan's door jamb that further infuriated him as he entered the office. Ryan looked up from his desk that had piles of manila folders and a mess of other paperwork. JD was going on about how he was a little put out that Ryan had not discussed these with him especially because JD had given Ryan a heads up that he was going to be talking with Perry. JD was upset that Perry knew more about what was going on at "The Final Result" than he did. Ryan stood up at his desk and asked JD what he thought might be the reason he would keep that information from him? JD not usually having a lack of words said "I don't have a clue that's why I am here asking you about it" Ryan said "Look before you have a heart attack, I did not tell you because I was not aware of these changes either"! They looked at each other and wondered what the hell was going on.

JD wanted to call Brian into Ryan's office and ring his neck. Ryan told him to settle down and rang Chuck at his extension. Chuck was now living in an extended stay hotel while he was looking for permanent lodgings. He was totally frustrated that he was stuck in this low rent hotel until he could take the time to look for a permanent residence. He had just flown back in after spending a couple days packing his personal belongings. Chuck was cranky and hoped this would not screw up his day because he wanted to spend most of it looking at downtown condos and a couple of house boats. Ryan explained the situation to Chuck including the relationship between Steve and Brian as well as Brian's interaction with Bill at PK that were definitely made repeatedly without input from anybody else above his pay grade. Chuck said Brian's actions did not reach the level of insubordination because he did not willfully go against any direct order and was in fact appointed to be the front man for communications with PK Enterprises. JD said he is making new rules that may negatively affect the cost of getting the product to market and besides he is as gay as a three dollar bill. Chuck stopped both of them and warned with an unnatural raised voice that having that kind of prejudice was illegal and he would not develop any strategy that would target an individual because of their sexual preferences. He continued on and quoted some recent law suits that cost company's million in settlements costs and additional costs in the way of negative moral for all employees. JD apologized and asked "what is it that you think we should do?"

Chuck said, "The best way would be for Ryan to bring Brian into his office and reprimand him for not running important decisions by him or you. I will witness the interview and you should just steer clear of the other situation for now". Ryan and JD agreed and JD went back to his office, banging his head again and swearing about it going down the hall.

Ryan called Brian and asked him to come down to his office. Chuck warned Ryan that he would say little or nothing in the interview and was there to just witness the interview. After Ryan breached the topic Brian immediately got very defensive and started to rant and rave about how much he had contributed to the company and he took it personal that Ryan did not have the confidence in him to make the decisions he had made. Ryan tried to assure him that the company did respect the contributions he had made but these decisions were out of character and frankly above his pay scale. At the very least Brian should have run the costly decisions by Ryan. In a real surprise move Brian said he would consider a separation from the company with a sizeable settlement. Ryan explained that was not where he was going on this and asked Brian to reconsider. Brian said he was going to clear out his desk and come back and see what they had to offer. Brian knew Ryan and JD had lost confidence in him and fumed around his office packing stuff up and shouting profanities out loud. Brian packed his stuff out to his car and returned to Ryan's office an hour after he had left.

Ryan had called Eileen and JD down to his office as soon as Brian had left. Chuck told the group that he thought Brian was just setting up a law suit and said he would go draft a release that Brian would have to sign to receive any settlement funds. Just as he was leaving Chuck asked Ryan to call him when they had an offer so he could enter it into the document. Eileen could not believe Brian had gone off, but started focusing on the fiscal issue of a settlement for him. The three settled on a 1 year severance package including benefits for a year and a buy out of his modest shares in the company. Norman had come over to Ryan's office with Eileen and could not believe what a generous package they were willing to offer Brian. He thought Jeez if Brian was getting that much how much was he worth. After all he was the Rock Star of the company and an Icon of the company from the very start.

Brian returned and barged into Ryan's office while JD and Eileen still were seated with Ryan at his small conference table. Ryan asked

Brian to have a seat and he responded "I'll stand". Ryan presented the deal and Brian said "fine when can I get it in writing and how soon would the funds be available". Ryan said he could get the documents and a certified check in about an hour. Brian stormed out and said he would be back in an hour. JD, Eileen and Ryan just sat there for a minute in disbelief. Chuck walked in to drop off the release that Brian would have to sign and left just as fast to prepare the settlement paperwork with the help of Missy. Eileen and JD left to go to the bank for the certified check.

The rumors were flying around the building that Brian was having issues but nobody expected him to leave, much less the speed of his departure, until then everybody thought Brian was part of the inner circle. As with many events in the corporate world people feel shunned when they are affected by a difficult decision. People think they should have involved them from the beginning and at the same time the people with real power make decisions without their input. Brian thought Ryan should have called him into the office and counseled him by himself. That would be great if everybody did not live in this litigious society. No one even counsels an employee these days alone without a witness. Like a double edged sword it makes the individual embarrassed and defensive. It was clear that Brian had some underlying issues and was quick to get defensive and caused his own demise. His demeanor displayed in leaving showed how big a chip on his shoulder he had. Brian even disclosed to a couple of people that he was being forced out because he was gay. However, JD, Ryan and Eileen vowed to treat each big decision carefully especially when it involved a key employee. JD had seen so many times over the years the cancer that grows in organizations where good quality people leave because they feel left out of decisions. Even worse many of them hang around and don't work to their potential after being basically ignored. JD had seen people so discouraged after years of hard work because a decision did not include their input.

Everybody is insecure, everybody wants something to love, and everybody wants to be loved. Individuals within an organization create the environment within the organization both negative and positive.

People support what they are part of creating. Many disgruntled employs leave through the side or rear door with a real chip on their shoulders. JD knew that the power was held at "The Final Result" by just a few individuals but he also knew that the momentum of the company depended more and more on the attitude of the entire work force as the company grew. The company was growing and JD personally re-vowed to make everybody at least think they were part of the company and had a vested interest in the success of the company. Decision makers often decide on issues based on their own interests and perceptions. They don't try to make a bad decision they just think and act without taking into consideration people's feelings. If the decisions cause good people to leave a company or not put energy into their work anymore, they consider it collateral damage. Normally they just think individuals will get over their hurt feelings and carry on. In most cases they do because they need the job to support themselves and or their families. This is the hold that many decision makers have on almost all employees. If they compounded what the loss of key employees or the lack of willingness to go the extra mile they would begin to act with more compassion, especially for long time employees. As is often the case it was not the decision itself that they were upset with, rather how the decision was made and that they had no input on the decision that was made. The bigger the operation the more likely this cancer will gain traction.

Owners that are also managers at a company are many times blind to thinking that everybody on the team cares as much as they do. The smaller the company, the less likely the cancer will take hold. But even in middle sized companies the owners surround themselves with individuals that they think can get the job done. The surrounding staff may indeed work hard and try their best to move the ball down the field. As time goes on members of the team vary because of their own personal individual complications in their own lives. They continue to depend on the company for family income. At a certain point they think losing their job or position would be intolerable. Many people then start to tell the boss what they want to hear. Of course the owners think "Good work is good life" and all the members on the team enable the ownership to think this because they want the boss to think they just love their job and the company as a whole. At that point it becomes the old scenario, "The Emperor has no clothes on". Norman hoped that Ryan would remember this and not separate himself to much from the actual work force and try to keep a perspective that people do have other issues they need to deal with every day after they leave work. A happy employee is one that actually feels like they are part of a team. Owners often times make terrible managers as they get to full of themselves and start thinking they are better than the average person and worse, start believing it.

Brian returned in an hour on the dime and the deal was signed in two minutes with JD as a witness. Brian left the building directly without saying good-bye to anyone. Nobody thought he would ever return to the building. When Brian got home he had a message from Chance on his home phone answering machine asking Brian to give him a call. Brian had expected to just live off his settlement for a while but decided to at least give Chance a courtesy call. He also wanted to know how Chance got his home number. Chance had liked Brian and knew he was smart. Chance was in New York when Brian caught up with him the next day. Chance said he had just pulled his Northwest manager for his holdings out there back to New York for a gaping hole in management at his headquarters in New York. He offered Brian the job and said "It will be great you can become the landlord for "The Final Result". Chance offered him a lucrative salary and benefits package. Brian had known and dealt with Chance's Northwest manager and knew the job would be a pushover for him with very little pressure. He could basically set his own schedule and would only have to manage one administrative assistant. She was already in place and had worked for Chance's operations for twenty years in the Portland area. Brian thought what the hell and told Chance he could start on Monday. Brian asked Chance how he got his home number. Chance said "I have my ways of getting information that could benefit me"

Steve continued to work well with Doug and threw himself into his chores but would never forgive Ryan for what happened to Brian. Ryan had a huge soft spot for Steve; after all, he had been shot in the melee surrounding the Denny era. Ryan had invited Steve to lunch in his office along with Eileen the day after Brian left the organization to try to clear the air. Eileen brought along Norman hoping to create a more comfortable environment. Missy had the lunch catered and brought it in at noon complete with a server. The waiter had come in and set up at 11 and lunch was served at noon. Steve was unimpressed and ate quickly and thanked them for their courtesy and asked if he could just get back to work. The schism between Ryan and Steve was now set in stone.

Norman thought what in the world; these humans are pretty thick sometimes. They have figured out that dogs react to and respect compassion and become loyal through constant consideration from their owner/partner. Yelling at us and or hitting us for bad behavior does not work. In order to train us properly they even actually have to care about us and yes love us unconditionally. Why in the hell do they treat each other with such contempt? Jeez, after all Eileen had her share of bad days and mistakes with him while he was growing up. He had long forgiven her for these deeds, even the time he had to fly in a pet cage in the hull of an aircraft with the luggage.

Why couldn't people just be at least civil with each other? Normal Norman never understood the whole "do whatever it takes" mentality and had watched and felt the hurt feelings, dead bodies and all the chaos that happens every day in most of the corporate world. The truth is he thought the people that act like this to other people treat animals even worse. He remembered an old war story JD told that had the boss actually say "Hey so the dog's dead just throw him in with the trash it's only a dog". He had another story about when his own dog died and he called in sick to handle the situation and his boss said hey its January in Maine just put him in the yard "he will keep till spring". Besides he said we need you in the office. JD did apologize to Norman for the entire human race each time he told one of these horrible stories of animal mistreatment. JD did love Norman and Norman appreciated that. Well sort of. People are people everywhere even given all the cultures. When they get treated badly they normally react badly and if they get treated well they normally react well. Wow- How profound Norman thought, they're thicker than I even thought...

Chapter 10

The Deadline

The Launch week was upon them and everyone was excited to say the least. Things where looking good and harnesses where actually coming off the line and getting transferred over to the distribution center and staged for the first pick up slated for April 18th. The first order of 15 was going to the store in Salt Lake. Ryan had brought in Jess MaCaan several months back. Jess was a well known Portland consultant that was renowned in the area for streamlining distribution centers to run the company's distribution center. He was a tough no nonsense Irish man that took nothing for granted. Ryan had mentioned to Jess that it might be fun to fly the first order over to Salt Lake in the jet. Jess responded with "so you don't want to test the system?" with a strong sentiment that Ryan just needed to leave the distribution to him.

Ryan and JD decided everything was in place to have a successful launch and turned their energy to getting some more customers lined up. Eileen sat in on a meeting with JD and Ryan and said that it was fine to leave distribution to Jess. Eileen went on and said "we are at or near capacity and would be again when the second line was on line in the fall. How exactly do you plan to service any other customers?" Ryan explained that JD had approached the neighbor that had the building across the street from "The Final Result" and they were interested in selling. JD had talked with both Perry and Bill at PK Industries and everybody thought it was doable to create a joint venture and buy the building. This was a 20,000 square foot; two story building that would double their space again. Eileen said "wow" and left to double check the numbers JD and Ryan where throwing around about additional expansion. As she left she told JD and Ryan that she had been working with Doug on getting a couple of additional dogs because poor Norman was getting worn out testing every harness coming off the line. He would never be able to keep up through the fall orders much less any additional expansion and or demonstrations.

As Eileen left she said they had found a perfect pair of boxers that where the same age (8) and where showing signs of hip distress. Their owner had died and the children did not want to keep them. As she closed Ryan's office door she said Hank and Oly would arrive on Monday and the company needed to figure out living situation's for the dogs and closed the door. Ryan and JD looked at each other and wondered how they were just put in charge of dog duty. Well, launch day came and went smooth as silk and everybody was getting excited about the launch party on Saturday. It had been a long haul, but the envisioned product was about to become a reality.

People where going way over the top with costumes and Missy had upgraded the music from a DJ to a 4 piece live band "Michael Levie and the Jackets". Perry and his assistant came in Friday night on "The Final Result" plane and were already in the Marriot ballroom when Ryan, Eileen and JD came by to check out the room about noon on Saturday. Perry thanked Ryan for the use of the plane and for the accommodations at the Hotel. Ryan said it was his pleasure. Even though, he did not set up any of the accommodations. There was Missy again, doing all the extra's, without much if any direction. What a pleasure it was to have her on board. Ryan noted to himself, tonight would be a great opportunity for some awards and promotion announcements. One of them would be to elevate Missy to "Chief of Staff". Missy was over at the catering department and rejoined the group and they went for a quick lunch. Eileen and Missy had never met Perry. Perry and Missy seemed to really hit it off. Missy was forty and Perry was fifty plus but it did not seem like they were even recognizing that fact. Perry really did not want to talk business he was in town to party. Perry's assistant kept fidgeting around his boss and Perry was starting to get perturbed that he was getting in the way.

Perry finally told him to go back up to the room and make sure all the costume stuff was in order for tonight. Ryan, JD, Eileen, Perry and Missy all ate a quick lunch. Ryan and Eileen may as well of ate lunch somewhere else, JD, Perry and Missy where in their own world. They seemed smug with each other, turns out it would be a wild weekend at the Marriot for more than just them. Ryan thought it was weird that Missy was so cozy with JD during lunch and Perry was acting strange too. Eileen thought maybe it was to make Perry jealous.

The event kicked off at 7pm and the band (dressed as the gang of YMCA) was playing light music in the background in the big ballroom at the Marriot. The room had high ceilings with great acoustics. This ballroom had a capacity of up to 400 people and it would be almost completely full that night. Ryan was scheduled to the podium at around 8pm. Missy wanted to wait till everyone had a chance to show up before Ryan addressed the group.

At about 7:45 Perry made his grand entrance, he was brought into the ballroom sitting in a makeshift rickshaw pulled by two behemoth men in Roman regalia. He also had two knockout, bountiful ladies fanning the rickshaw on either side. They where scantily clad with what looked like Egyptian outfits leaving little to the imagination. You could not even see Perry but you sure knew it had to be him. He had been planning this for a month and even had the two men and two women drive up from San Francisco with all the costumes on Friday. The group that was surrounding Perry was all from a cast of characters that had just finished a movie shoot in San Francisco. As Perry emerged from the rickshaw the crowd began to applaud, Perry had a professional makeup artist "do him up" and he looked remarkably like "Wolf man Jack". The band immediately broke into "Midnight Special" (Wolf Man Jack's signature song). Perry even got up on stage and did a rendition of "My Girl" himself, looking mostly at Missy, but finished greeting the crowd with, "Let the Ever Loving Light Shine on You". Perry had asked Missy at lunch to give the band a heads up to play the song when he arrived. Missy had also changed the seating at the head table so she was seated between Perry and JD. Perry had been practicing for weeks on his impression of Wolfman Jack, he was giddy as he took his seat at the head table. His entourage sat at a table directly behind the head table, the table was hastily set up by housekeeping, directed by Perry's assistant after Missy had left at 5 o'clock to dress for the evening. Missy was surprised and a little perturbed about this extra table when she arrived back in the ballroom. She was no longer surprised or upset after Perry made his entrance.

Perry was by far the one that went way, way, way over the top but everybody else went a little over board too. Just at the head table alone you had Wolf man Jack (Perry) - JD went as (Kenny Rogers)- Becky had the best Disco outfit portraying (Donna Summers)- Ryan was dressed as (Jim Morrison)-and Eileen being more than 5 months pregnant went as (Mama Cass) wearing a free flowing 70,s style moo-moo. Missy was stunning in her (Cher) outfit including the very low neck line. What a wild looking head table. Terry had asked Missy to be seated at a table separate from the main table with her family along with Doug and his new fiancée and Steve. Steve had asked Brian to come but that was not going to happen. Terry was still a little shy to attention even though she had mostly recovered emotionally from the Denny debacle. Terry, her husband and four kids came as the (Partridge family) and actually won the best costume prize, they fit the portrait perfectly. Doug and his Fiancée Julie came as (Mork and Mindy) and they looked hilarious. Steve rounded out the second table trying to look like (Bob Dillon). Eileen got the message of defiance that Steve was trying to present, and was sure that Brian put him up to it. Steve would leave shortly after the presentations were made. Steve was very uncomfortable in any social environment when he was alone, especially in this one.

Ryan approached the podium and asked the band to take a break and come back jamming with the best they had. Missy had planned for the event to end around 10pm. Ryan began by thanking everyone in the room for their hard work and the successful launch. He then asked everybody to turn their attention to the ballroom doors in the back of the room. The band was instructed to bust into "The Best is yet to come" by Frank Sinatra. Norman was pushed into the room on a cart four feet off the ground by a hotel staff member and he was standing in full Harness with a smart looking neckerchief holding a vintage 70,s Frisbee in his mouth. The entire crowd gave Norman a standing ovation all the way to his place at the head of the main table. Missy had even brought in a big spotlight to use just for when Norman made his entrance. Norman's entrance was just as impressive as Perry's, and he looked great for his years seemingly puffing out his chest as the cart rolled up the main aisle. Ryan went over and gave Norman a big hug and then returned to the podium. Ryan once again asked for everybody to turn their attention to the back doors and in came Hank and Oly the new test dogs for the organization, led by Steve and Doug. They got applause but Norman felt good that nobody was standing up as they had done for him. Hank and Oly sat next to Doug and Steve respectively while Norman stayed lying on his perch between Eileen and Ryan at the head table. Doug and Steve both had taken one of the dogs to live with them. Doug picked Oly and Steve took Hank.

Ryan then covered a few important announcements. First of all he said, "we now have confirmation from our shipping company that all 200 harnesses have confirmed tracking numbers and the first harnesses where on the shelves in the PK store in Salt Lake City." Ryan then publically thanked Jess for his hard work and expertise to get the product to market. He then told the crowd what Perry had told him just a few minutes before. "We also have confirmation that two of the harnesses have already been sold in the Salt Lake City store. Two out of five on the very first day they hit the store." The crowd roared with approval! We are on our way yelped Ryan. After letting the audience settle down he continued thanking all the board members individually for their contributions. The seating at the head table had Ryan sitting next to Perry then came Missy, next to her JD, then Becky, and Eileen next to Ryan. After Ryan got through with some lengthy thank you's, JD got up and took the microphone from Ryan and asked the crowd-could we ask for a better leader than Ryan Oxbow? The crowd shouted back in unison NOOOOOOOOO! JD went on roasting Ryan a little and listing his many contributions including being the founder of the organization. JD finally relented and gave the podium back to Ryan.

OK Ryan said, and thanked JD for his kind words. We have even more good news he said. With Perry's help setting up the joint venture we have now gone to escrow on the building across the street and should close in 90 days. Ryan said that this new building will house the new demonstration area to do presentations for prospective customers. He went on to explain that going forward we will fly prospective customers in commercially for future demonstrations. For that reason Ryan informed the crowd they would not be renewing the lease on the plane. There would be no reason to continue with that expense. Perry had told Ryan he would pick up the lease and if Ryan ever needed it for something he could just give him a call. Ryan told the crowd "Just a couple more announcements and they could get on with the festivities." He announced that JD was going to go back to half time and Eileen was going to do the same thing at least till after she had the baby. They will share the Chief Financial Officer duties. One or the other would be on call at all times. Ryan then announced Missy's promotion to his Chief of Staff. We have realigned our corporate structure once again and he revealed a power point chart on the overhead monitor's in the ballroom that displayed the line chain of command.

> President, Chief Executive Officer
> And Chairman of the Board-Ryan

Supervisees
> JD and Eileen-co Chief Financial Officers
> Terry- elevated to Chief Operating Officer
> Becky- elevated to the Treasurer
> General Council-Chuck
> Chief of Staff-Missy

Supervisees'
> Doug – director of research
> Steve- director of manufacturing
> Jess- director of distribution
> > Board of Directors

Chance-501 shares
Ryan – 240 shares
JD- 139 Shares
Eileen- 120 shares
Terry, Becky and Chuck with 20 shares each.

In his final action addressing the group Ryan asked Terry to come up to the podium. Ryan had warned Terry that he was going to call her up to the podium but did not tell her why. Ryan explained that they had one award for "Employee of the year" and Terry had won that award, the first ever for the company. Ryan once again asked the crowd to turn their attention to the back doors. In came a cart that had a bronze bust of Norman that stood almost a foot tall and a foot wide. Hotel staff pushed the cart to the podium with the spot light on it all the way. Terry and her family were very touched even though it had been a very difficult year for all of them. Terry only addressed the crowd briefly with a thank you and returned to her table and got hugs and kisses from her family. Norman thought "NOW THAT'S AN AWARD". Ryan then said to the group "Let's have some fun" and the band struck up the first dance song of the evening, YMCA.

The evening ran long as almost everybody was still dancing and having a blast at 10 pm when the band was suppose to quit. Instead Missy had them play till 10:30 after Ryan closed the party out at ten by grabbing the microphone one last time to thank everybody once again and say good night for the evening. Perry invited most of the guests to the Marriot lounge across the courtyard for a night cap on him. JD, Missy, and Perry, where all at the bar until well after midnight laughing and telling stories about their past. Missy did not even make it out of the building that night as she spent the night in Perry's suite, or at least that's what everybody thought.

Ryan, Eileen and Norman stopped by the bar briefly and headed home around 11. Ryan actually proposed to Eileen that night. When they got home Eileen walked in the living room to find two huge vases of roses of six different colors. In between the two vases was a line of lit candles leading to the bedroom with rose pedals on either side of the trail of lit candles. The sweet smell of roses combined with the essence of the candles brought Eileen to her knees and she began to cry like a baby. Ryan sat with her on the carpet and started crying too. She of course said yes, but again demanded to not have a ceremony till well after the baby was born. Ryan had arranged with a neighbor to have the candles lit when he texted them as they left the party. Norman thought "Man this is pretty cool" and then lit out the doggy door to give them some privacy.

Charter 11

The Marathon

Monday morning May 3rd started the post deadline era at "The Final Result". With everybody wearing t-shirts handed out by a still blurry eyed Missy at the front door and Doug handing them out at the manufacturing entrance. The T-shirt had Norman's picture silk screened onto the front in full harness with the words Normal Normans Helping Harness and the date on the back. The magenta T-shirts with white lettering were now the company colors and were replicated on each harness package. The moral was high but there was a ton of work to get done over the next four or five months.

It was a great Northwest spring day in Portland in the seventies and sunny. Many people where eating lunch in the small urban city park across the street from the manufacturing entrance. Norman looked out at the people in the park while eating lunch with Eileen and thought "wasn't it great to see all the people happy and displaying his picture" All was right with the world Norman thought. Most of Norman's duties now revolved around the training of Hank and Oly. They were catching on fast and where now doing all of the testing work. The rest of the time Norman normally could be seen roaming around the complex at will and offering comfort and happiness to the atmosphere wherever he went. Hank and Oly; where now almost completely adjusted to both their new home life, and their work life. Both dogs where playful every morning but became focused when called upon to perform. Hank especially could work all day and still want to play with Oly before everybody went home. Oly on the other hand would get his work done, but if it was a heavy regiment day he would be pretty tuckered out. Doug and Steve lived separate lives away from the company but Hank and Oly had a special bond between each other because they had lived together in the same place for almost 8 years. The "dudes" (as they had become known at the company) normally hung out together all day, 5 days a week. Doug had not wanted to take both dogs on at home but after several months he did end up with both dogs since he really had the space for them at home. Steve did not like leaving Oly home in his condo even though he had made elaborate accommodations for Oly including a pet sitter most of the time if Steve and Brian where gone. It was hard for Steve to give Oly up, but he knew it was in his best interest.

Once again "the dudes" could hang together 24/7/365. Doug had a nice 5 acre parcel out in Gresham about 10 miles east of company headquarters toward Mount Hood. Doug was gradually building a home himself on the acreage, but currently only had the apartment over a garage livable. He did have the entire 5 acre parcel fenced so "The Dudes" had a great place to hang all the time. Doug's house plans where pretty elaborate and he had recently changed the plans to better accommodate special places for "The Dudes" to hang. In the apartment Doug routinely had the discovery channel on as he was reading and "The Dudes" seemed to love watching it, as all three of them hung around the wood burning stove in the apartment. Doug even cooked all his meals at home on that same wood burning stove, as he had not seen the need to put a real cooking stove in the apartment. He planned to use it as the studio after he finished the house so it did have a bathroom but not much of a kitchen. In reality Doug was just cheap and had a hard time using up any amount of cash for nearly anything. It will turn out that Hank and Oly are out of the picture before Doug would finish his 4000 square foot home. Norman thought "Jeez a baby sitter for a grown dog-how ridiculous"

Eileen was busy as JD had called in and said he was going to be out of pocket for at least a week due to pressing business in New York on a private matter. Chance had attacked one of JD's other interests because he had lost traction on anything with "The Final Result". JD arrived in New York to a subpoena at the airport to be present in court the following morning. Chance had worked with elements of a big union to try to unionize a small work force that produced machined products in upstate New York. JD was co-owner in the machine company that had just five employees. It never seemed worth it for the Union's to try to organize this small outfit but with Chance pushing and their own enrollment faltering badly they got 3 of the 5 employees to sign unionization cards. JD knew at this point that it was a full tilt union campaign with these 5 employees'.

The subpoena was for unfair business practices and named both principle owners. JD 's partner Chris was also the one that managed day to day operations for the little company that produced solid but low profits for the last decade. JD had only supplied the seed money for Chris. Chris tried to sweeten the pot for the employees after the union was involved and that was a big no no with the federal officials. There was a vote date set and JD would be in New York for at least 10 days till the vote took place. JD managed to delay the proceedings for unfair business practices until after the vote date. After that it would be a mute point either way. Finally Chance was showing his inner darkness. The big union would have not gone after such a small company that had no other workers to go after beyond the original 5. As it would turn out Chance was considerably mobbed up with the underworld in Northern New Jersey. JD found out from some family friends that had ties to Northern New Jersey that Chance had ordered the union drive on the small company. There are not that many people that can just order a unionization drive on the small independent company.

JD hung around operations for a week trying to gain some leadership over the work force. He feted out that the new hire Chris had been put on just two weeks before the cards where signed was a plant by Chance. Chris was pretty unsavory in a social way and was no match for Chance and a plant with the backing of a global Union. JD had known a couple of people on the work force and wanted to know their grips. They had very few and where just pawns on the chessboard. The vote did take place and the company won 4 to 1. The only vote for the union was the original plant who resigned after the vote was taken. Big waste of time and energy for everyone involved and showed again how vindictive Chance was. It was obvious he had no idea of giving up the rampage to cause as much chaos as he could for "The Final Result". JD and Ryan where now significantly scared of Chance. JD had information from a government source he had worked with in the past that one of Chance's operations was involved in financing pirates off the African coast for a big cut of the bounty. JD asked him "why is he not under arrest". The agent from the central intelligence office said "He is very good at covering his tracks" JD did not share that conversation with Ryan. Chance was scary enough for Ryan without that little tidbit.

Eileen was working with Terry to start the financial spreadsheets on the expansion. There was some heavy lifting for her to figure the upcoming costs. At least she had real income to forecast for now and had the money to pay cash for most of the parts needed to get the original production line back up and producing. The second line invoices that would facilitate the doubling of production where starting to come due and Terry as well as Eileen wanted to make sure they had the ability to pay those costs with current income from PK Enterprises. They always got the balance sheet out every month but it had voodoo projected income lines that until now would have been hard to defend to any accountant type.

Meanwhile Ryan was trying to brainstorm how he could expand the customer base. He re-started conversations with the nation- wide organization that supplied wholesale products to veterinarians across North America. VSNA (Vet Supply of North America) was interested and had called Bill at PK Enterprises to see how the product was moving. Bill told them that initial projections were being met and even told them they expected to place additional orders as soon as the company had capacity to fill the additional orders. He told them he was not in a position to give them actual sales figures because the product had only been on the shelf for a couple of weeks. In reality most of the PK Enterprises stores had literally sold every harness in stock and had back orders placed that would exceed next month's shipments.

Bill called Ryan after he talked with VSNA to give him a heads up on what he told them and to make sure he knew the harnesses were going like hot cakes and asked if there was any way to ramp up production. Ryan was taken aback about the sales numbers and told Bill he would assess what could be done and get back to him by the end of the week. Ryan called a board meeting for Monday morning May 10th and personally called each board member to make sure they knew its' importance. When he broke the news to JD, Ryan felt like someone hit him over the head with a 2x4-he was actually seeing stars. JD knew better than Ryan or anybody else what could come next. Ryan asked JD if he could fly back Friday so Terry, Eileen, JD, and Ryan along with Chuck could work over the weekend to have a plan for the entire board. JD said he was beat but would catch the red eye back tonight. Later Ryan saw Becky in the hallway and asked her to join them for a weekend retreat at Timberline Lodge on Mount Hood. Ryan was starting to realize he would need all the perspective he could gather to find the path ahead for the organization.

The weekend was a long 2 day 12 hours each day marathon that stretched everybody to their limits. Missy had been collard to keep the notes for the meetings and Perry and Bill, at the request of Ryan, flew in on Saturday night and joined the group for Sunday's session. It was evident that the team needed to develop the new building much quicker than they had imagined. Bill explained to the group that he had pressured the seller to close by July 1st about 3 weeks before the original deal was to close. But Bill also said the seller had agreed they could go in and start renovations right away. The real up side for the new building after renovation was it would allow the company to produce 800 harnesses a month at full capacity. That would allow the company to produce up to 1200 harnesses a month. Perry said he would up his orders to 600 a month and that would allow 600 potentially for new customers. If the VSNA came through with an order everybody concluded they would take at least the lion's share of the 600 and leave again the need for more expansion. The concern turned toward whether the company could handle the costs of expansion. Perry brought up the fact that he would be willing to issue small loan amounts at extremely low rates in case cash flow was needed during the future expansion.

On the dark side, Chance had been waiting in the wings for some time to make a move on the company. Chance had lined up a hedge fund group, one that he was an influential board member of, to make an offer to buy the company. Ryan and JD suspected as much when they got notification that Chance would be at "The Final Result" board meeting on Monday. They decided as executives of the company that they would ward off any take-over attempts by Chance and his group. Ryan felt comfortable because he now and always did, trust JD and Eileen and he did not think Chance could sway Becky, Terry, or Chuck to vote in favor of whatever Chance brought to the table.

Chuck warned the group that Chance could bring pressure in a number of ways. Eileen had already informed at least JD and Ryan that Chance or one of his subsidiaries had already bought up many of the loan notes issued to "The Final Result" including somehow the unsecured loans from governmental agencies such as the small business association. Even with all these Ryan did not think Chance could hurt the company even if somehow he could get all the loans called for full payment. The wild card Chuck said was the original building lease, because of the restructuring of the company during the same time the lease was signed, Chance could file a suit to get that lease expunged and put a new not so sweet lease in effect. This Chuck said could be fought in court and tie it up for at least a year and that would bring the company to a new lease anyway. JD said remember Chance is still the person with the most shares in the company and I don't think he will try that because he still had a good sum of money at risk and the rewards for him would diminish if he just tries to throw shit in the way of the company.

However, JD did add that Chance no doubt has a plan to try to get control back of the company. Perry also got his two cents in saying it was possible Chance might just try to kill the company out of pure spite and take the loss and write it off on his other holdings. Perry then added you people are sitting on a crop that could blow the socks off anything else he has seen in 20 years and you are trying to refuse to water it. What you need to do is, buy or build a separate manufacturing building and make the new building only administration, demonstration and distribution. He followed by saying the large square footage needed for the future is going to be in the manufacturing end. Administration and distribution would grow but not at the pace manufacturing will grow. If the demand pans out to be as grandiose as everybody thinks the demand is going to be an ongoing problem forever. Perry was now intense and said you could say good riddance to the building you are in that Chance owns. Besides, you should be calculating what you would save by not moving all this equipment to several buildings and have three different buildings producing some of the product. Economy of scale will tell you that having all the manufacturing under one roof would pay off in the end. Perry then stood up and said he and Bill had to go but he would be willing to buy or build a facility and lease it back to the company with a stout lease or buy or build a building and take a majority stock position in "The Final Result". As he was departing he addressed the group and said "if you can't find a way forward I will try to get it done myself-this is too big a deal to walk away from and let die on the vine". Ryan walked Perry and Bill to the conference room door at 3 pm Sunday and Perry told Ryan separately to call him early Tuesday morning. Perry also assured Ryan he would do anything he could to help. The group took a break and decided to come back at 5pm for one final session.

Norman and Eileen where walking around the lodge at the break and Norman thought-man all this majestic landscape and everybody is not even looking at it much less relishing its beauty. These folks are pounding through life and it is just going by in a blur for them and they are not seeing any of the beauty that surrounds them. Yup thought Norman sometimes those humans are pretty thick. The beauty is way different when you are walking than when you are driving, it is much more intense. There is a time to focus Norman thought but you have to slow down sometimes to see the beauty that surrounds you. This was the first time Norman had worn the harness in the snow and it worked great for traction. A good side effect which no one thought to market, not yet anyway. Norman wondered what a military harness would do for dog patrols around the globe, search and rescue operations-man the sky is the limit. I think I agree with Perry Norman said to himself-water the shit out of it and see how big it can grow.

It was late spring but Mt. Hood has glaciers that people ski on year round. Eileen and Norman just sat at the base of the Glacier chair lift and watched the skiers and snow boarders make their turns down the mountain. Too soon, Ryan called Eileen back to the meeting.

The group gathered again at 5pm and needed to finalize a plan on how to handle Monday's board meeting. The group agreed that they would fend off any take-over attempt. They also would put a motion to move to look for an additional building that could house the entire manufacturing operation. Building would be ideal but would take too long given the remaining lease on the current building runs out just 7 months from now. JD and Terry will be appointed to find and secure a separate manufacturing building within 60 days. The future was scary and murky for the company now, and Ryan knew he would have to will many individuals to stay the course and continue to take the risks of expansion. Norman was ready to go home and get back to a regular routine. Normal Norman was a year older now and was doing great but liked to nap more and more. The group concluded their last session just before 7pm and Ryan invited everybody to have dinner at the lodge together before they all headed home for good night's sleep, hopefully.

Chapter 12

The Attempted Hold-up

Monday morning May 10th came in with a roar as Ryan called the board meeting to order at 9am in the new conference room at the new building. It was not quite finished yet but Ryan thought it would be a good environment for him, and not so good for Chance. Ryan had had a contractor come in and remodel the conference room space over the past weekend and get the space at least usable. The doors were not even hung and the electrical cover plates still had not been put in. The room smelled of fresh sheetrock and paint but the carpet and lighting were installed and they had new plush expensive leather chairs and a massive walnut meeting table. Missy had a continental breakfast catered in for the morning session and everyone was seated around the large round table.

Ryan called the meeting to order and asked the group to hold all new business till after the agenda items had been addressed. Ryan explained to the group that the demand for the product appeared to be outpacing any production level that the company currently had or any production that could be accomplished with this new facility. Ryan went on to propose a motion for the company to acquire a 40 to 50 thousand square foot building with the express use as the entire manufacturing location for the company. Furthermore, this has to be operational in six months. After a moderate question and answer period the board voted and the motion passed with Chance being the lone no vote. Several other legal and budgeting motions also passed that supported the expansion to yet another building. Timing would be essential and Ryan explained that this move would negatively affect the organization in the near term but would solve the manufacturing output issue for the long term. JD and Terry where appointed to put their entire focus on the new acquisition. Eileen would have to look after the accounting for Terry until the building was acquired. Becky would have to take over all the financials issues for the short run. Ryan concluded that was the completion of the agenda items and asked if there was any new business that needed addressed? Chance, who had not said a word during the entire session stood up and requested the floor. He addressed the group and said he had a prolonged presentation and said "seeing that it was after 11 am and I would prefer not break up my presentation I would move that we adjourn for lunch and reconvene at 1pm." Ryan agreed and ended the morning session.

Ryan brought the meeting back to order just after 1pm. He gave the floor to Chance and what ensued was one of the rockiest and boisterous presentations that even JD had seen. Chance started off by chastising the entire board and told them none of them deserved to be on the board and most of them should not have even qualified to be a board member. Chance specifically attacked Ryan and said he had no confidence he could lead the company successfully. He then made a motion to relieve Ryan as CEO and Chairman. He got no second from any board member, and the motion failed as he suspected it would. He then offered Chuck, Becky and Terry at the board table 100,000 thousand dollars each for their shares. Thank God Chuck and Terry where not in it for the money but it did get a raised eyebrow from Becky. In the end none of them was interested in teaming up with Chance. He then offered an even more ludicrous offer for their shares. Chance was red faced now with a vein popping out of his neck the size of a large fountain straw. He was spewing saliva out of the side of his mouth and looked like a crazy psychotic's patient on a tantrum.

Ryan took the floor back and asked Chance to sit down and take it easy. Chance did sit down and asked for a 5 minute break to compose himself. Missy had staff bring in the 3pm coffee and cookie trays early and everybody took a 15 minute break. Norman left and was headed back over to Eileen's office. He could not take anymore and was worried that he might attack Chance and rip him a new ass.

Norman thought as he meandered back to Eileen's office with Missy, if there was ever a person that needed two ass holes it was Chance.

After the session was called back to order Ryan asked Chance if he had any other motions the board needed to act on. Chance said yes. He proceeded to open his briefcase and throw what appeared to be 3 law suits at Chuck. One was what they suspected, to throw the old lease out and replace it with a lease that had the going rate, four times the current lease. The second was a suit that was against all other board members for competence issues. He was asking for compensation at well over two million dollars for his as he put it, compensation for the company's largest share holder that had no say in corporate matters. The third was against Ryan, Eileen and JD on similar issues. Chance then notified the board that he was calling all his company notes that he now held. This amount was just over three hundred thousand additional dollars. He then closed his briefcase and said he would entertain a payment of 2.5 million dollars to settle all points. He went on and said the dollar amount was not negotiable and he would take action on all fronts next Monday if he had not heard from the company by then. Chance turned and gave the board the bird as he left the conference room. What a class act, JD yelled as Chance was walking out the entry opening were the conference door would soon be. Ryan turned to Chuck and asked if any of the lawsuits had any meat to them. Chuck replied "two are frivolous but the building lease suit may have some standing". However, he said they will all cost money to defend. Ryan asked Chuck how they should proceed. Chuck said he had had preliminary discussions with a local law firm to take up the lease issue if it came to that. "Looks like it has come to that" Chuck said. He continued that he would work on some legal delays himself on the other two law suits and let the Morgan, Wholestein and Wholestein law firm take the lead on the lease law suit. They will file for a continuance with the federal court by the end of the week. Monday will come fast Chuck said and he wanted to take every precaution so Chance did not have a way to shut down operations or even try to evict the company in some sort of legal maneuver.

JD then piped up and said "can we offer Chance the payout he asked for and shape the payout over a 10 year term"? Terry said that it was possible but it would be a heavy load for the company to bear. Ryan had another idea and wanted to talk to Perry and discuss the options. Ryan quickly brought the meeting to an end and told everyone it was likely they would have an additional board meeting Friday so he said "keep your schedules free for at least the morning on Friday". Ryan explained to the group that he would take the rest of the week and work on options himself with JD. Ryan requested the rest of the team to buckle down and concentrate on their independent duties. This event can't negatively affect the rest of the work group Ryan stated. Ryan took the rest of the day off and went out to Hood River to kite board and release pressure and take some time to think about how to approach Perry in the morning. Ryan had used the escape to kite boarding and before that with wind surfing for almost two decades now. The wind in his face and that exertion it took to do his kite boarding was a way Ryan could clear his mind and focus on one objective.

Ryan got to the office early Tuesday morning and had not got much sleep so he was pressing now. In the past when he pressed himself like that he tended to make mistakes. He recognized that but also needed to give Perry some time to mull over the new situation. So at 9am he placed a call to Perry and explained the happenings at the board meeting and told him that he wanted to take another day himself to consider all the options but also wanted to get Perry's noodle working on the problem. Perry responded with "I have an answer to the problem right now" Ryan told Perry that he did not want any long discussions on the matter today and asked Perry if he could call him early Wednesday morning. Perry said sure but he would not change his opinion overnight. Ryan got JD and went to his car and proceeded to drive again to the Columbia River Gorge with his kite surfing gear. The weather was pleasant for the middle of May and the wind was up, gusting at 35 knots. Ryan wanted JD's complete attention and the hour drive each way would give him that. All the way to Hood River JD went through a slew of options on how to handle the Chance situation.

Ryan dropped JD off at The Gorge Hotel and told him to have lunch and he would be back in a couple of hours. Ryan told JD he wanted his best solutions to the situation not more options when he returned. The Gorge Hotel was a very high end historical hotel in the Gorge and Ryan knew it would be a good place for JD to formulate his best plan to go forward. The hotel had beautiful grounds including a 200 foot waterfall that emptied out into the Columbia River. JD wondered around the grounds for an hour before he went inside to have lunch. The hotel only had 39 rooms but the restaurant and bar were enormous. 20 foot tin ceilings adorned with elaborate etchings. The hotel also had banquet facilities that could handle parties of up to 200. JD wondered why he had not even heard of the place just 45 minutes from Portland. JD was disappointed that he had not heard of it because he fancied himself as somewhat a student of historical places and the hotel had been listed as a historical building two decades ago. What a destination place just 45 miles from Portland and only 35 minutes to the slopes on Mount Hood.

Ryan returned to the Hotel around 1pm and just ordered a salad as he sat down across the table from JD. Ryan said, "Come to any conclusions?" JD said well we can't just pay off Chance and still finance a new manufacturing complex. JD continued that Terry and Eileen along with Becky could probably keep all the plates in the air at least for a while but at some point the cash flow situation would dictate the company would end up dropping a plate or two. JD told Ryan he had seen company's try this many times before and he would not encourage a settlement with Chance that would put the company in a poor cash flow situation. Ryan said fighting him would be very expensive. JD replied that at least those costs could be spread over many years. OK said Ryan I am going to call Perry in the morning and get his "so called" answer to the problem and he would like Eileen and JD to be in his office at 10 am. They said almost nothing about work on the hour's drive back to Portland. Norman had come along as he had so many times over the last decade on a trip to the Gorge. Norman loved the scenery both up and back on Highway 84 with its high rocky cliffs shedding beautiful waterfalls into the mighty Columbia River.

He use to range up and down the beach in Hood River unleashed and playing in the shallow water while he was waiting for Ryan to get his turns in on the river. Eileen often joined them too but being almost 6 months pregnant she had declined for at least the last four months. Norman now, mostly meandered around the beach waiting for Ryan with his leash on and in full harness but still managed to get completely wet and of course roll in the sand. All the way home JD complained about the wet dog smell in Ryan's car. Norman thought to himself TUFF! Deal with it BIG guy. JD did say as Ryan dropped him at the office "see ya Norman I still love ya even though you smell to high heaven" Norman looked at Ryan as they drove home and gave him the "Like I give a hoot whether JD like's me or not" look .

Ryan got to the office about 8 am and was going through reports and trying to figure all the angles before 10 am. Eileen and Ryan had breakfast together and JD had already put his final two cents worth to Ryan via e-mail so Ryan now had all the information he was going to have before he called Perry. Ryan had already decided that his first line of defense would be to offer Chance full payment of his demands over a 10 year period. Chance had said the amount was not negotiable, but he did not demand a specific term. Ryan hoped the offer would at least lead to some negotiation talks and delay any action on Chance's part. Ryan called Chuck down to his office too and he and Eileen and JD where all positioned around the speaker phone at Ryan's small little conference table in his office at 9:55 am.

Ryan placed the call to Perry and once connected explained to Perry who was in the room. Perry said fine I have Bill here with me also. Ryan asked Perry in kind of a rye diction "so what is the answer to our problem with Chance" Perry came back abruptly as always with "it's simple I will just buy out Chance and take his share and position in the company" JD started to scratch his ear as he did when he is either confused or pissed. Eileen and Chuck where trying to process the statement in their own minds. Ryan responded "well that would solve the problem all right" Perry said "well what else are you going to do"? Ryan explained that he was going to offer a pay out to Chance over a ten year span and that would give the current officer's the control they were looking for. Perry responded with "Yes you will have control but have a negative cash flow at least for the next few years" Bill stepped in and said "this kind of thing hanging over a company is exactly the kind of thing that kills companies, sometimes in less than a year." Perry additionally warned that doing that would put your whole organization at risk. Bill actually spoke up again and said with the current joint venture on the new building and the ties PK Enterprises has with "The Final Result" was a marriage made in heaven for Perry to be in the position that Chance currently holds. The discussion went on till almost eleven and Ryan told Perry he would call him tomorrow after the board meets to let him know which way they were going to go. Perry said fine but we are burning daylight and a decision needs to be made as quickly as possible. Perry finished with a stern statement that he had other opportunities and would not wait very long before he would pull the trigger on the funds he was prepared to use for a "The Final Result" deal and put them into another project.

Friday morning came and all board members, except for Chance, were in attendance at the new conference center at the new building at 8am. Ryan opened the meeting and explained the options to the group. After much confrontation and mashing of teeth the group agreed to at least make a run at paying off Chance. JD asked Ryan if he thought he could keep Perry on board as a back -up position. Ryan said he would ask him for some commitment along those lines this afternoon. Ryan instructed Eileen, Terry and Missy to work with Chuck and come up with the paperwork needed for the offer to Chance today and get it fed-xed Saturday delivery to Chance so he has it in his hands before Monday morning.

JD wanted Ryan to go out with him today and look at a couple promising buildings for the new manufacturing center. Ryan concluded several other minor issues with the board and officially closed the board meeting. All members left except JD and Ryan placed a call to Perry. Perry was disappointed with the decision but said he would stay in queue in case the offer was rejected, but made sure Ryan knew that it was not an open ended dateline. Perry said if we don't have a deal by the end of next week he was going to move on another opportunity that would use up any budget he had set aside for this deal. Ryan said OK talk to you next week. JD and Ryan left for lunch and to look at the two buildings JD wanted for the manufacturing complex. Ryan also drug Doug along to get his input on the locations. Everybody took the weekend off from what had been a grueling regiment in the last several weeks. All the board members hoped that Chance would take the deal. The company would be wounded but had at least a chance to recover from the wound. Norman thought over the week-end "Hope is not a plan"

Monday morning May 17th came in like a bad dream. At 8:30 am Missy was served at the office with a court order to stop all operations and desist from any correspondence from or to any company employees to any outside individuals. Missy frantically called Ryan down to the lobby. She was concerned that Ryan was going to lose it all together when he hit the lobby. She thought to herself "why did I not just run away 10 days ago when someone asked me". Ryan was reading the court order and asked Missy to get Chuck down to the lobby. Chance really had the rails greased to get a court order severed at 8:30 am on Monday morning. To top it off Brian was there representing Chance with two local police officers on either side of him. He had a big shit eating grin on his face that incensed Ryan.

The court order was the result of the suit on the so called "bogus lease agreement". Missy returned to the lobby and told Ryan, Chuck was not in yet. Ryan barked at her to get him on his cell phone. One of the police officers told Ryan that operations must stop immediately and nothing could leave the premises and she can't call out to anyone anymore. It was obvious that Chance never intended to make a deal. He was going to any extreme he could to get Ryan removed and or separated from "The Final Result". If his actions killed the company Chance was willing to risk it. Just as Ryan was about to explode Chuck came through the lobby door with Alan Wholestein of Morgan, Wholestein and Wholestein legal group with a different court order from a federal judge that over road any court order to stop operations issued by a county or state judge. By this time JD had joined the group in the lobby and thought-Jesus H Christ how does this shit happen in separate courts before 9am on a Monday morning. Norman wandered by and had some morose thoughts about how society has got to the point of being such a litigious society. He said to himself "don't they understand the only ones that win are the attorneys" Once again Norman was thinking how humans can be so thick. After calling in the sergeant from the local precinct it was determined that the order that Chuck and Alan had trumped Brian and Chance's and operations could continue.

Chapter 13

One Long Hot Summer

Operations did continue and "The Final Result" had shipped all their May quota's already and where working on June's orders. The projected production was a low estimate and as it turns out they could produce almost twice the 200 projected. This was good and welcome news because having empty shelves at PK stores would make the demand go down in both the short and long term. Without enough presence at the stores the momentum of sales would be lost too. It would have been hard and possibly impossible to recover the chemistry that was currently driving sales.

Doug and Steve were now focused on fine tuning the current manufacturing process on the current line because they had not been allowed to start a new line in the new building. They both were also helping put the finishing touches on the demonstration pavilion being built in the new building. Hank and Oly had ongoing training in the new pavilion and were about ready to show the harness to new or prospective customers. Norman thought the new digs where a little over the top including a viewing stand. He did however, give it "two paws up" because it could efficiently display the harness and still give the performers adequate space to perform. Norman thought okay you two "I paved the way for you guys, don't screw it up" Norman could come across as a surly bugger sometimes, but he had a huge heart and was proud of how well both Hank and Oly where doing in their training.

Ryan and JD were on the phone with Perry Tuesday morning to explain the events of Monday. Perry said "that figures, where you going from here?" Ryan did not want to give into having Perry become the largest share holder in "The Final Result" but saw no other viable answer. JD had already conceded that it was the best way forward and pushed Ryan to make the deal. JD pounded away at Ryan telling him the board will approve this, and it was the only way to get Chance out of the way. During the conference call they all danced around on the specifics, but in the end a deal was struck. Perry said he had one final demand. Ryan asked what that might that be at this stage. Perry said he wanted to present the check to Chance in person. "Nobody had a problem with that" Ryan said and added after we get the paperwork done we will overnight it to you. Perry said he would fly commercial to New York and cash out Chance next week. Perry said that he was sending Bill up to Portland to work with JD on the new manufacturing complex. Bill had extensive experience on real estate deals and could make things happen fast. Perry told Bill to take the plane as he was going to fly commercial to New York.

The company needed to move fast now as any holdup would affect the already hamstrung manufacturing infrastructure. The deal was consummated and Perry was in transit to New York on Thursday May 20th. Needless to say Chance was enraged at what was transpiring. Chance went into a furry when Perry reminded him of what transpired 20 years ago In Salt Lake City. Perry was up in the face of Chance and said "what goes around comes around". Chance was not going to back down and told Perry "we will see who is standing in the end". Perry said this is the end for you at "The Final Result". Before Chance stomped away he told Perry "This is not over".

Chance would file all sorts of law suits after this but from now on he would go down as a large footnote in the company's history. Chuck even had to put a new lawyer on the payroll to handle just the correspondence on the flurry of law suits and paperwork Chance kept filing. Ryan even had to declare Chance or any of his employee's personas non-gratis at any company location. Chuck was able to get a restraining order against Chance or any of his employees to stay 50 feet away from any company location. Chance still hired private server companies to deliver new lawsuits. More than once Chance had acquired assets from companies because of timing and filing of paperwork. Chance and his group of bandits were masters of taking advantage of legal maneuvering. Chuck was committed to not getting hammered by missing a filing deadline with whatever court Chance and his group filed in. The number for Chance's lawsuits now stood at six. These suits were filed in three different venues. Again trying to find a loophole or opening. JD privately asked Chuck to not depend totally on the new attorney to deal with legal issues with Chance. Chuck smiled and said "he is fresh out of law school and I need him for reference and brief work. Don't worry I have him on a very short leash". Chuck was a little put out that JD would even ask him that, but he knew JD just wanted to not have to worry about the new guy getting clipped by some gunslinger Chance would throw at him.

JD, Bill, and Ryan had settled on two potential buildings as sites for the new manufacturing complex by the end of May. Perry flew back from New York to Portland Friday May 28th to look at both buildings with the group. Perry was feeling pretty good and satisfied to finally get some restitution from Chance after more than 20 years. He was ready to do anything to keep the new status quo in place for the foreseeable future.

This new building was going to be another joint venture and would fuse Perry and "The Final Result" at the hip. Either building would work so the priorities became cost and location. One building was a little further away than the other building but was newer and would require less upkeep over the next decade. Bill was hot on this newer building because he had spent so much money on PK enterprises buildings in the past when they thought they were getting a deal. He brought up some statistics on how much cheaper the newer building acquisition would be over the long term. Perry and Bill had formed the PBREJ limited Liability corporation with Ryan and "The Final Result" to buy the last building. This new building would also be under the same umbrella corporation PBREJ. The organization had Perry funding the down and closing cost and "The Final Result" would be responsible for paying the mortgage. Ownership would be split 50/50 with buyout options for the "The Final Result" over time. The group decided to make an offer on the newer building. The building was completely empty and had no leans on it so everybody thought they could get a speedy close and take possession by the end of June or early July. After a somewhat drawn out meeting with the principle owners of the new building, a deal was struck "in kind" and Contingencies included building inspections and funding confirmation.

The building came back clean and the funding was in place because Bill had totally greased the wheels and closing was set for Monday July 2nd. Bill did however negotiate that "The Final result" could occupy the building immediately with a short term lease back from the current owners for 45 days. It ended up that the two entities would just merge the short lease into the closing agreement so that the lease cost would be amortized over the term of the loan. Taking possession was important so delivery of hardware that was scheduled be delivered to the administration building could go direct to the new manufacturing complex. The new complex was about 7 miles from the administration building but was at least a 20 minute drive on city streets.

Ryan and the board had a quick meeting on Monday July 9th and decided on several issues that had to be dealt with immediately. Eileen was just a month away from going on maternity leave so all financial responsibilities where going to go to Becky. JD wanted to concentrate on new customers but still could be available to Becky for advice. So the board voted Becky to become the new CFO. Ryan would remain president and CEO and still be Chairman of the Board. JD was elected Director of new affairs and he had "dancing ferries" running around his head about the possibility for an upcoming IPO. That was always JD's end game. He wanted to cash out big with "The Final Result". This was the first time JD or anybody else really believed "The Final Result" could go public. Eileen would remain a board member. Terry would continue to operate the business and take the position of COO. Perry was nominated, though he was absent, as the new banking officer and become a board member. Chuck would continue as general counsel. All motions passed.

Ryan told the board he was going to put 100% of his energy into the building of the new manufacturing complex and asked everyone to run whatever questions they had on operations though Missy and she would be the one to determine whether to bring it to me or not. Ryan even took a small office at the new manufacturing complex and would work out of there until at least late fall with Doug. Doug's office in the new complex had plenty of room for two and Doug planned to be on the manufacturing floor most of the time anyway. Ryan knew that if he went to the administration building each morning there would be many days that he would get caught up in day to day operations and never get a chance to get to the manufacturing complex. Missy also was elected as secretary for the board of directors and she would also continue her duties as Chief of Staff. Norman wondered "where the hell was this new building" I haven't even seen it. He thought do we even have the capability to grow this fast?

Administrative operations would move entirely to the new building including demonstration teams, R&D, legal, accounts payable, accounts receivable, data entry, distribution, and all other office staff. So the only thing left at the old leased building would be the old manufacturing operation and hopefully that could just be moved to the new manufacturing complex after the lease was up in November. The moral at the company was running high by mid July and the future seemed bright for "The Final Result". The summer flew by for all of the employees and the company was flying high. VSNA the vet association came on board with new orders. JD had several other potential customers already through the new demonstration pavilion. Wall Street had taken heed of "The Final Result" now that the company was going to be North America wide. Investor groups where starting to hover overhead to see if there was a way to steal the company and its intellectual property. Sometimes there is a window of opportunity to get in on the ground level of this kind of technology before proprietary rights diminish over time and ultimately competition is able to duplicate the technology. The key to success was to be first to market which "The Final Result was, but now the company needed to get infrastructure including distribution in place that could solidify and support the demand. Eileen had asked Ryan if a community group could rent a small place in the new building to start a shelter for homeless dogs and cats. Ryan had agreed to house the group at a rate of a dollar a day for the first year. Norman thought, well it looks like they are going to continue to improve on the company's core initative to make society better.

Ryan had not seen Hood River to windsurf for 3 months. It was now the end of August and the initial manufacturing line in the new complex was actually pounding out product. Eileen was two weeks away from her due date and was now spending most of her time on bed rest. Hank was testing at the new facility and Oly was doing all the testing at the old facility. All systems were a go and Terry, Missy, and Becky had a pretty good handle on day to day operations. Doug, Steve, and Jess had the manufacturing and distribution moving in the right direction. The biggest challenge was to continue building out the new manufacturing complex to the point it could take over the volume of harnesses the old facility was still producing. This had to happen by the time the lease ran out November 1st. Most if not all the hardware and parts from the old manufacturing building would still have to be dismantled and moved to be used for spare parts in the new operation. Norman started hanging around the administration building again as Ryan had moved back into his office in the administration building. Norman liked the time he spent with Ryan at the new manufacturing complex and the pace at the new facility. Norman seemed to have almost a vocabulary with both Hank and Oly. He actually loved seeing them work. These dogs have a purpose Norman thought. They have the dignity to do something worthwhile, and the satisfaction that it is a noble cause and a contribution to society. Most Humans would relish that kind of opportunity, but no doubt few would recognize it. Norman sure understood that.

In preparation for the baby coming Ryan had asked JD to be on hand the first two weeks of September to be in place while Ryan took a few weeks off to spend at home with Eileen and the baby. September 5th came and Eileen went into a 16 hour labor birth and they had a baby boy 6 pounds 5 ounces with everybody doing fine. When Ryan and Eileen brought young Ryan home Norman thought "rut-rough this may be a problem" By the end of September Ryan was back on board and raring to go. Ryan relished the first week off with Eileen and the baby but grew weary of the daily grind of domestic life by the second week. Ryan had so much going on in his brain and so many worries about the company that Eileen after ten days said "you need to go back to work NOW" The company had now grown to over 100 employee's and was getting to be a pretty big octopus with all the usual complications of a small to mid- sized company with a huge potential to grow.

The first day back, for Ryan JD asked him if it was possible for them to take a long 3 day weekend get away with Perry and Bill. Ryan asked JD what was up. JD said the Wall Street pariah were still circling and sooner or later they would try one way or another to gain at least some sort of position in the company or as they normally like – completely take it over. JD said he tentatively had some principles from Wall Street firms scheduled to meet with them so they could get some idea of what they propose so they could develop strategies to ward off take-over attempts. Ryan thought that was smart and at this point he would welcome anything to give him a break from changing diapers for a week-end. What are the dates, and where are we going Ryan asked? JD asked can you manage the second weekend in November. Ryan said he could and asked again where are we getting away to? JD said Perry and Bill where going to bring the plane and they could ferry whoever needed to be brought to and from the meeting from the airport. Again Ryan asked, "were the hell are we going"? JD said he was finalizing some reservations and would tell him that afternoon. JD then proceeded to leave and would not return till Thursday afternoon November 13th.

Ryan had talked to JD and exchanged many e-mails during most of October but JD kept avoiding the location and said he had not yet firmed up all the reservations and logistics. JD just kept complaining about being completely buried in other personal issues in New York. Ryan even called Perry and Perry said all he had was the time frame and to fly in Thursday night for the weekend. Hum, Ryan thought to himself. Wait a minute JD was not big on details and he would not have all these big wigs coming in unless he had everything nailed down. Ryan then asked Missy to come into his office. Missy said she was sworn to secrecy. Ryan said, "You work for me tell me where we are going. "Missy said with all due respect, "I am not going to tell you" and asked to return to her duties. Ryan threw up his hands and said "whatever you are dismissed". Ryan thought to himself "when did I lose control" Norman thought it was awesome that JD was keeping the location a secret-kind of added to the anticipation. JD and Perry were the only ones that knew who the players where that where going to be at the meeting. JD, Missy and Perry where the only ones that worked on the "who and the where" of the meeting. This was not the first or last time these three would keep people in the dark.

Chapter 14

Destination Pirates Cove

Ryan, Terry, and Chuck boarded Perry's plane after it landed in Portland. JD and Missy had flown over to the secret location with Perry and Bill earlier. This was the second of many ferry flights this weekend. The second group whisked off to the undisclosed location. The pilot JT was a great pilot and loved working for Perry. He had wide experience on this particular jet and even trained other pilots on the eclipse aircraft when he was not flying for Perry. He explained that he had just dropped Perry, Bill, JD and Missy off at the destination and told the group it would be about a 35 minute flight. Off they went East bound toward Mount Hood. When they landed Ryan did not recognize the terrain but it was a private dirt air strip somewhere in Eastern Oregon. The weather was pretty socked in both Portland and during the flight so it was hard to tell where they were. As the jet rolled up to the small out building at the airstrip Ryan recognized Bill standing outside a black SUV. As they piled into the SUV the plane turned and took back off on its way back to Portland. Norman stayed home this trip with Eileen and the new baby, but boy he would have liked to explore the grounds around the private estate the group was about to experience.

As the SUV powered around the last curve from the airport on a dirt road the massive lodge seemed to appear out of nowhere. This place was a full blown working ranch spreading out as far as the human eye could see. With the hilly terrain it was hard to get an idea of how big this place was. They drove slowly up the final drive, boarded by white six foot fences on both sides with a heard of Bison on the left and a herd of Heifer cows on the right. The main lodge building was enormous, with several other buildings surrounding it. As the group unloaded, Perry appeared on the porch at the top of a 20 step stairway that was at least 20 feet wide with rocks and waterfalls on both sides. Perry raised his glass and yelled "welcome to Pirates Cove". The group smiled and waved, but most of them had no idea of what was about to transpire including Ryan.

As the group moved through the front door of the lodge and entered the expansive entry rotunda it was apparent that this place was something very special. A man that apparently was in charge was welcoming everybody and making sure he shook hands with each person. He then addressed the entire lobby in a resounding voice and introduced himself, as Milton Freewater the caretaker for Pirates Cove. He was dressed in a sharp western button down shirt; Carhartt vest and blue denim jeans and Tony Lama cowboy boots. JD had warned everyone to bring warm casual clothes for the weekend and it looked like a pretty laid back environment. One of the reasons Missy chose this place was its western charm. She thought this would be an alien environment for Wall Street types and give JD and Ryan some kind of advantage mentally if it came down to serious negotiations.

Milt explained that cocktails where at 5pm sharp in the library and dinner would be served at 7pm. Until then he said the lodge's in house ranch hands (7 of them) would get everyone settled into their digs. "Everybody is free to take a nap or just freshen up and there are a ton of activities all in and around the main lodge. All the guests are welcome to do whatever they want anytime. There will always be a staff member close to open the bar, pool, spa, or the bowling lanes if any of them happen to be closed." Milt however did remind everyone that this was a working ranch and recommended that if anyone wanted to roam around outside they needed a ranch hand escort to be sure everyone was safe. The check in procedure was to distribute keys to the guests along with a 9 by 11 inch map of the grounds and that was it. On the reverse side of the map was a schedule for the week-end.

Friday-
    Check in -free afternoon
    Cocktails at 5pm in the library

Dinner in the dining room at 7pm

Movie in the lounge at 9:30 pm (optional) tonight's film "Misery"

Saturday

Breakfast 7am to 9am in the dining room.

Morning fly out-8am fishing (optional)

Noon –Lunch in the dining room

1pm to 5pm –Workshops –lobby and library

Dinner 7pm in the dining room

9 pm – bowling tournament-lanes off the lounge

Sunday

Breakfast 7am to 9am in dining room

9 am till 3 pm-workshops in the lobby and library.

Deli lunch available in the lounge at 11am till 1pm

3-6 pm -Fishing (optional)

As everyone from "The Final Result "were getting settled in and exploring the lodge, the plane continued flying in groups of people. Each of these groups was housed in the outside cabins around the main Lodge and had separate meeting rooms attached to each cabin. The ranch was specifically designed to house corporate events and they did not miss a link in accounting for any individual or group needs. As Ryan was walking to his room with JD he asked "who the hell is paying for all this?" JD said "don't worry its covered." JD then said he was going to the spa and then back to his room to take a little nap before cocktail hour. Ryan said he would do the same and would see him down at the spa in about half an hour.

Ryan entered his room and found no TV, Radio, or even a clock. The room was laid out to be a working office but had no electronics. Ryan grabbed for his phone and saw "searching for coverage". Ryan changed into his spa cloths including the most lushest embroidered robe he had ever felt with a note in the pocket that said "take me home I am yours". Ryan stopped by the lobby counter to inquire if he could have cell coverage or internet access for the weekend? The house ranch-hand said there was one satellite phone available in the lounge for emergencies but nothing else. Ryan moseyed over to the lounge and called Eileen to make sure she knew she was not going to be getting any texts, voice mail or e-mail over the weekend and to give her the satellite phone number. It was an emergency for Ryan so Eileen would not panic.

As Ryan entered the spa area he was amazed at the size of the complex. The pool alone had to be 30 by 60 and then there were male and female locker rooms, two huge 8 man hot tubs and another whole area with a series of individual claw foot tubs. Three massage tables were set around the pool in small thatch covered huts that could be draped off for privacy. The spa attendant asked Ryan if there was anything she could do for him. Ryan said no I am just going to have a swim and maybe hit the steam room. JD joined him for a swim and then had an hour massage scheduled (with drapes closed) before his nap. Chuck and Terry where taking an outside tour of the grounds with one of the ranch hands. Missy was sitting with Perry on the porch. It was a brisk November afternoon but the clouds where breaking up and the view from the porch was beginning to reveal how big and bountiful this place was. Perry liked his perch on the porch because he could size up each group as they arrived. There were 4 groups of people that arrived for the weekend and Perry recognized or knew about half of them. Some of them would come over and shake his hand and others would wave or nod at him as they entered the lodge. Bill was in his room panicking about how he was going to handle each individual group and their proposals. Each group had anteed up 25% of the cost for the weekend not including the shuttle cost of the plane that Bill would bill them for.

Everybody was gathering in the lounge around 5pm and started to introduce each other, have a tasty beverage, and just mingle for the first hour. Ryan was beginning to understand that this was not a brain storming environment, it was a sales seminar, and his company was the sales target. Ryan cornered JD at the bar and said what are we doing here?" JD said, "We don't have to accept anything but let's see what they each bring to the table-otherwise we will never know." JD was 58 and had 3 kids that where all done with college and spread throughout the country. His agenda was beginning to be totally the opposite of Ryan's thought process on the future of the company. Ryan was still going up, up, and away in his mind for the company, but JD was beginning to want to see what his cash out could be. JD had some big deals over the years, but he could now smell real cash on this one. This deal could be the one that could put him in a position not to worry. This kind of cash would allow his kids and his grand kids not to have any financial worries ever.

Three of the four groups where either Wall Street representatives of private investing funds, private equity funds, or hedge funds. The remaining group was an insurance conglomerate group from Atlanta. This final group specialized in the takeover of small state of the art companies with very high potential of demand future. This Atlanta group had the most potential for a good fit with "The Final Result". All the groups had at least two attorneys', some of which were also officers in their respected company. Each group had at least one bean counter and one lead negotiator. During cocktails and dinner the individuals continued to introduce themselves to each other and renew some past contacts. No specific business was discussed Friday night, as that had been agreed to previously by all groups.

Everyone retired from dinner to the lounge. The lodging staff started the movie early as Missy had suggested at 8:30. Even though no one had set up what movie that was to be shown, it did set the tone of mystery as well as cruelty and pointed out that many times in life circumstances are not what they seem. Ryan was kind of freaked out by the movie because he envisioned that he was the one that was about to be tortured. Strangely the investment types were cheering during some of the most gruesome parts of the movie. JD and Perry sat next to each other during the movie and spent the evening studying the individuals reaction to what was going on in the movie. Perry prided himself in being able to pigeon hole certain personalities and use that knowledge during future negotiations. Perry had done this for many years as had JD and it had often paid off for both of them. They both knew by the time the movie was over who they would pay the most attention to during the workshops. For these two they had it narrowed down to two groups to concentrate on during the workshops Saturday. If you are wise enough to listen you can categorically determine who has quality in their communication and who is just a loud mouth that tries to overcome inadequacies with volume. Two groups showed those ugly tendencies during cocktails and the movie. Those two groups where out of the running before the workshops even started. Norman would have picked those two groups out too. Missy and Bill did not attend the movie but instead retired to Bill's room to go over some logistical details for tomorrow's workshops. Everyone else retired after the movie and well before midnight.

Nineteen people showed up early for breakfast wanting to get in on the morning fishing trip. Bill, Becky, and Chuck were the only ones that stayed behind and those three worked on what financial information they were actually going to share with any of the groups during workshops. Breakfast was quick and the group headed for the airstrip by 7:45. When they arrived at the airstrip there were six small Cessna planes staged for takeoff. Milt was leading the group and actually piloted one of the aircraft. The other five pilots worked and lived on the ranch and where either ex bush pilots from Alaska or had become pilots while in military service. The planes took off one by one with Milt leading the pack. After a 15 minute flight they landed at an even smaller airstrip on the edge of the Columbia River next to the tiny town of Rufus, Oregon. It was just a short golf cart ride from the planes to the boats that where staged on the river bank. Everybody loaded up the boats and the pilots of the planes became the captains/guides in the boats. The groups where on the water by 9am in hunt of the massive bottom fish in the Columbia "The Sturgeon".

After two and a half hours on the water two of the boats had landed one of the prehistoric looking Sturgeons. The water was starting to whip up from East winds that had continued to get stronger. Milt gave an order by radio for all boats "return to shore". By 12:30 everybody was back at the lodge eating lunch and showing the pictures of the fish, the ranch rule was catch and release. Even though both where large enough to be taken by law. Milt explained they liked to release them so the next group will have a chance to catch em. Both sturgeons weighed in excess of 50 pounds. Milt estimated both fish where between 50 and 60 years old. "Man", said Ryan "these fish have been swimming 60 miles of river between the two Dams for more than 50 years?" It seemed unimaginable but it was true. "These bottom feeders have to be one of the ugliest fish on the planet" JD said out loud to the group as they finished lunch. He went on further and tongue in cheek said "HOPEFULLY WE WON'T SEE ANY BOTTOM FEEDERS OF THE HUMAN KIND THIS AFTERNOON" This was the first shot over the bow to the investors to bring their best proposal. Perry had suggested that JD somehow set the stage just before the workshops started. JD's timing and statement were perfect to set the stage for "The Final Result" to get to the bottom line quickly.

Perry felt fortunate to be associated with all the principles of "The Final Result" especially JD. Over the years there is always an individual that stands out above the crowd. Many times in the past Perry was the person standing above in a deal and never really had a partner that he could trust to be the front man for an important deal. Ryan thought the statement might be a little arrogant and mentioned that to Perry. Perry said "with this group you need to be as crass as you can be-that's the only way to handle these sharp shooters". Remember Ryan, Perry continued, "These people are ruthless and they don't have your best interest at heart". We need to handle these people like we where tending to a group of sharks that are all in the same small pool. As Perry and Ryan headed off to the workshops Perry gave Ryan the following advice "Put your helmet and Kevlar on Mr. big shot we are entering a war like environment where the opposition would eat your young if they get a chance". He ended his advice by saying "for Christ sake let JD handle the negotiations with these people he has dealt with these types for the last 20 plus years." Ryan's head was now spinning around like a top.

The workshops began at 1pm and "The Final Result" group spent about 40 minutes with each group to explore proposals of what their group would be willing to offer up. All three groups from New York had deals structured to have the parent or new company completely take over operations and buy out everybody involved, they did offer just minor positions to the present organizational structure. This was not only operational positions but also on controlling positions at what would be a new company. The buyout amounts being talked about where amazing. This was turning out to be a real life changing event that could affect everybody at 'The Final Result" individually.

The Atlanta group took a different tact with a proposal that was not as lucrative in buy-outs but could be a plan to have the current principles still in place from a control standpoint. In their proposal "The Final Result" would become a solely owned subsidiary of the proposed new company but would retain management rights. Their proposal would leave the current principles in their positions and they would retain control of the company operations and guide the company in the future. All groups recognized the product would be going global soon. If any of them could land it, it would be a home run deal in any arena. In order to justify the amount of pay outs that were talked about they used world-wide sales projections that supported the kind astronomic buy-out amounts. All teams had given their best shot and the workshops where finished for the day. Everyone was in the bar after a long day before dinner. "The Final Result" group including Bill and Perry would skip the bowling tournament and met in a late night special session in the library at 8:30 pm.

Bill held the floor for about an hour in the late session summarizing each proposal believing he had it whittled down to two to consider. One was the Atlanta group with strong ties to two huge insurance concerns. The other New York group was willing to pay exaggerated prices to cash everyone out but would demand of course complete control of company. Ryan and JD would receive just stupid money and so they both said they needed to at least sleep on it. JD suggested the group convene again for lunch at noon on Sunday to decide on anything or nothing. JD asked Missy to set up a separate lunch for them in the library on Sunday. "The Final Result" group headed for their rooms at 10 pm, exhausted.

Sunday morning at Breakfast JD notified two of the groups that there was no need for any additional presentations and he let them know they would have the plane at their disposal all morning to get them back to Portland. Of course the two groups leaving had already been selected by JD and Perry before they had given their presentations. At 9am the remaining New York group made one more aggressive run at a takeover considerably increasing their offer over night. The amount of money being discussed was crazy, but there it stood on the table. The Atlanta group stuck to their original offer; however, they had an additional proposal that detailed the money involved for the principles of the company when and if the new company had their first IPO. It all finally became clear to even Ryan that the New York group was going to get the future IPO money if they made their deal and would most likely sell "The Final Result" to the highest bidder even before an IPO was offered. At 11am JD invited the final two groups to have lunch in the dining room and the company would have an answer by mid-afternoon.

Ryan opened the meeting in the Library promptly at noon and tried to summarize the final two offers. He was struggling with the massive numbers and asked Bill to clarify some of them. After an hour or so Perry spoke up and said "Look, if we are really going to entertain the New York groups offer I would like to have the same opportunity and do the buyout myself and make all the future IPO money," JD, Chuck and Becky were leaning toward the New York offer mainly because of the upfront money involved. JD even said "look I have given everything I had to this company the past couple of years and I want to cash out". After all JD had originally hoped he would have limited time and work load on himself and instead got a two year full tilt sprint. In the end Ryan and Perry had the will and the power to influence Chuck, Terry and Becky to vote for the Atlanta plan. JD was pissed but did understand, he would have to wait to cash out big. Ryan asked Perry to go and give the news to the New York Group as JD was now in grump mode. Ryan also asked Missy to invite the Atlanta group to the lounge to toast the deal. Ryan had Eileen's proxy and the board voted 5 to 1 to adopt the motion to accept the Atlanta groups offer. Before Ryan adjourned the meeting he said he was going to restructure the current company one more time before they accepted the deal.

It was obvious now that the second distribution center would be in HOT-lanta. Bill, Perry, JD and Ryan had previously discussed this possibility and had approached Bill to become an officer for "The Final Result" and head up the Atlanta operations. Bill had already eagerly accepted the offer as he was originally from Atlanta and his folks where getting up in age and wanted to be close to help them out. Bill would report directly to Ryan in Portland. JD informed the group that he was resigning from any position at the company but would remain a board member. Eileen had already done the same thing as she wanted to stay home and have one more baby. Becky would stay on as the CFO at double her salary with an additional bonus options for stock. Terry would also remain in place and run the Portland operations again doubling her salary and additional stock options. Chuck would remain General council with a healthy raise and with bonus stock options. Bill was nominated and approved as a new board member, and given 20 voting shares in the company. Perry would remain as the largest share owner and continue to be Vice President for banking as a title although he would only take the 50, 000 dollars a year as a board member. Perry really wanted to only have to attend the required 10 board meetings a year. He had plenty to do and would leave the day to day operations to Ryan and his trusty brother in law Bill. In a final move, at the final board meeting as a separate entity, Ryan invited two people to join them from the Atlanta group. Ryan nominated and the board approved them as board members. Perry and Ryan knew even more arm's length board members would have to be brought in before any IPO could happen.

Tom Newhouse and Wayne Wooster from the Atlanta group came in beaming and excited about the deal. The motion passed and the group moved to the bar to hoist a few. The Atlanta group headed for the plane around 3. The plane would have to come back and ferry Ryan, Becky, Chuck and Terry back to Portland and return once again to pick up Perry, Bill, JD, and Missy to head back to San-Francisco via Portland. The future was about to move on down the line. No one had signed up for the afternoon fishing trip. As JD stood on the porch with Perry, Milt came out to thank them for coming. JD said "sorry about no one going on the afternoon fishing expedition". Milt gave Ryan a wry smile and said "We always put that on the schedule but no one usually goes. After the decisions are made at these things the winners and losers all want to go their separate ways."

Chapter 15

Betty Davis Eyes

When Ryan got home and explained the weekend to Eileen she was totally okay with what had transpired and actually happy that Ryan along with everybody else was not individually liable for the company's performance and obligations anymore. She was beaming from ear to ear and Ryan wrote it off as being happy because of the deal. Little Ryan was trying to roll around on the floor going from side to side. Norman went back to in front of the fire after greeting Ryan. Norman thought it was a while ago that Ryan had lost control of the expansion and this new venture would be good for all concerned. Norman was content with napping around the house and the daily walks with Eileen around the neighborhood. Norman wore his harness just on walks and on the now rare public appearances. After a great home cooked dinner of roast beef, mashed potatoes, and asparagus Eileen was able to get the baby down to sleep. As they sat on the couch alone she told Ryan she was pregnant again. Ryan said "Jesus Christ what more can happen for me" Ryan finally let loose after holding back his emotions all weekend. He cried like a child for 15 minutes. Eileen said "I hope those are tears of happiness" he replied "you of all people know that they are". They discussed briefly getting married again that night but decided that it could wait again till after the baby was born. Ryan thought Eileen's mother will just have to bitch about them living in sin for another year.

Monday morning November 17th marked the day of the beginning for the new Entity now known as Normal Norman Helping Harness Inc. Most of the marketing already carried that name and image. So "The Final Result" would soon be defunct as soon as the paperwork got signed and attested to. As Ryan sat in his office he added up what amounts of payout people would be receiving and wondered what it would do to some people. Oh so right he was. The principles would be paid additional monthly bonuses based on the amount of shares they owned and the volume of sales produced. This was in addition to still retaining their current shares. JD and Eileen also would receive an additional 250,000 plus 6% interest for their original investment also in the form of a bonus. Perry and Ryan hoped that these monthly bonuses would help retain key people. The deal initially would devalue their stocks because roughly 51% of the share values would now be held by Normal Normans Helping Harness Inc. now known as NNHH. Everybody agreed that that would be a great "Ticker Symbol". These Initials would work great for corporate identification in general and be easy for correspondence. The big money was still down the road a bit when the company would go public. Norman thought "how much money does anybody really need"? After much reflection the truth finally appeared to Norman in a dream during one of his many napes that Sunday evening. "It does not have anything to with needing money. It has all to do with how much money individuals WANTED".

JD and Missy sauntered into the office around noon going straight to Ryan's office. Ryan knew something was up as he had never beat Missy into the office ever, much less her coming in at noon. JD explained he was not mad at what had transpired he was just in the space in his life where he wanted to totally cash out. Ryan looked at both of them and asked "what's up"? They looked at each other and JD said they had just leased a villa on Grand Cayman Island for a year with an option to buy. JD had put up the money for the lease but put both their names on it. He intended she would own half the house if they did indeed agree to buy it after the first year. Ryan said "how long has this been a plan and what was the deal with Perry?" JD explained that Perry had agreed to go along with the ruse, as they both thought it would be better to not bring that drama into the company when so many things were going on. Missy had got so use to using Perry as a replacement name for JD she had often used it even when she did not need to.

Missy told Ryan she was now way more comfortable leaving because he would have a great staff and line support with the new entity coming on line. She was exhausted with her duties and longed for a getaway on the beach to recharge her batteries. She had worked almost every day for more than 20 years, many of them 60 hour work weeks for the last 10 years. She thought if she ever got a chance to get out she was going to take it. This was her chance and she was taking it. JD and Missy made their rounds at both buildings saying good bye to everyone. Everybody was amazed that they kept this a secret as long as they did. Usually in the corporate environment the rumors fly around all day every day. But these two had so much miss-direction going on with Perry's help that nobody saw that coming. Nobody but Norman that is. Norman had caught them many times in an embrace thinking no one saw them. Norman however, thought it was nobody else's business and kept that secret to himself all this time. When JD and Missy were leaving the administration building around 2pm JD told Ryan to give him a heads up on the December board meeting now set for the second Friday of each month for NNHH. Hope you have it in Hot-lanta JD said loudly. JD shook Ryan's hand firmly and said "you know I am still just a phone call away". Ryan turned and gave Missy a long hug and said "I will miss those Betty Davis eyes." So many times Ryan had seen those eyes look right through people and get people to do what she wanted them to do without having to say "do it." "Not everybody has that kind of talent" Ryan told her. Ryan wished her the best and told her she would be badly missed.

As JD and Missy drove away Ryan sat down on the bench in front of the main entrance to the Administration building. He began reflecting on the happenings of the last almost two years and tried to get himself centered for what was to come. Geez he said to himself "I am the last man standing" Eileen, JD and Missy would now essentially be gone from day to day operations.

Becky and Terry were the only other original board members from when they started this dicey venture. Becky was thrilled with her position of CFO because of the challenge ahead to take the product global. Terry would run the day to day West Coast operations and take the title – Director of West Coast operations. Bill would take the position of Director of East Coast operations. Chuck would still hold the title of General Counsel. Becky, Terry, Bill and Chuck would all report directly to Ryan. Perry would still base himself out of San-Francisco and he and Ryan where both now in search of administration assistants and or private secretaries that they could trust.

Doug and Jess would end up moving to Atlanta to develop possible future manufacturing and distribution for the East Coast operations. Steve had lost most of his sour grape attitude and was making more money now as Director of Manufacturing for West Coast operations than he ever thought was possible. After Atlanta operations come on line the NNHH would have over 200 full time employees. Ryan wondered whether he could make good on his long ago promise to himself to contribute to a noble cause and not try to force people to do something. Rather, to have the work force want to contribute to the company. With this big an octopus it was going to be impossible to keep control over operations. It was time to start managing with the knowledge that you do not have control. Ryan left the office early that afternoon just to drive to the Columbia River Gorge with Norman. If was not kite boarding season but he just wanted to walk the beaches with Norman with a crisp East wind in their faces.

As they walked Norman thought "Geez big man, take it easy on yourself, you have been through a lot over the last two years and came out as the king of the hill". Ryan looked into Norman's eyes as they sat on a big log on the beach. As he did he re-realized that eyes are always the key to the soul. Ryan recounted the times when he looked into someone's eyes in a key situation and somehow the answer appeared in his mind. Norman looked back into Ryan's eyes and said to himself "you are FINALLY starting to understand you have a special gift". Norman continued to think "the eyes always give you the answer". It's just that most of the human race is afflicted with the Human Thick Brain Symptom (HTBS) in dog talk. Ryan, thought Norman, is one that may have chance to break through the mental barriers of the mind. In a final push Norman tried to telepathically send Ryan a vision of the future. The future is always uncertain but Norman knew Ryan would need to always move forward especially when it feels like you are barely able to put one foot in front of the other. Ryan would have to be able to envision the moves well before they happened at the new company. Ryan somehow got the message and asked how the hell was he going to be able to do that? Norman replied "Just like you envision the turns and jumps you do on your sail board before you even hit the water."

This was not the beginning nor is it the end for any of the principles at "The Final Result". The future will not have "The Final Result" as an entity but the individuals within the now defunct entity will continue to experience their own passions. The past did not have "The Final Result" as an entity, but the individuals involved all had foundations that somehow resulted in these people creating "The Final Result"

Many of the observations and narrations in this book were brought to you through the eyes, ears and mind of "Normal Norman". It's a dog's world; we humans just live in it.

The End-For Now